Enchantment

Enchantment

A novel by LINDA GRACE HOYER

HOUGHTON MIFFLIN COMPANY

BOSTON

Second Printing c

Sections of this book have been previously
published in *The New Yorker* and *McCall's*.

———— for John and Mary—

Dear eyes of delight, dear youthful tresses, foreheads
Furrowed with age, dear hands of love and care —
Lying awake at dawn, I remember them,
With a love that is almost joy I remember them:
Lost, and all mine, all mine, forever.

John Hall Wheelock

AUTHOR'S NOTE

Enchantment was begun at the suggestion of Rachel MacKenzie of *The New Yorker* magazine. It is to her encouragement and continuing concern that I owe the completion of this book.

CONTENTS

Enchantment

_i_ ───

A HALLOWEEN STORY

WHEN HANS WAS SEVEN (almost eight), he handed me one
of the oblong pieces of cardboard that sometimes divide
cereal boxes and said, "It's a Halloween story, Mom-mom.
Everybody wrote one in school today." And, on the long
side of the cardboard, in lower case letters somewhat larger
than the letters that follow, I read, "The Bad Witch."

Since witches had been spoken of in whispers by the
adults who lived in my grandmother's house when I was
seven, I repeated the title to Hans in a whisper that was

really a question with overtones of dismay. "But how could you, Hans? You've never seen a bad witch."

"Read my story, Mom-mom."

Hearsay had it that it was customary for our most superstitious neighbors to barricade their front door with a broom lest my grandfather, passing it on his way to the mill, might bewitch one of their children.

Of this phenomenon, however, my father, who invariably whispered when family conversations turned to sex and money, had not spoken in a whisper. "The evil eye" was a laughing matter and not to be confused with the disciplinary power that he had, from time to time, recognized in his father's gray eyes. "The Minuit look, when Uncle Tom gave it to you, would *move* you to do what he had asked you to do." It was a gift that heredity had shared not only with Uncle Tom but with my grandfather and his only son, my father. And, unlike "the evil eye," "the Minuit look" was to be taken quite seriously. It is a way of regarding one's vis-à-vis that I have not inherited and Hans — after two generations — has. So I read "The Bad Witch" and, with the author's permission, quote:

"There was a witch and she liked to turn boys and girls into *bad* boys and girls. And one sunny day she turned a boy into a real bad boy. Such a bad boy that he killed the witch."

After praising Hans for having told his story with a minimum of obscurity, extraneous detail, or, indeed, any of the faults that my story will have, I said, "Hans, did you know that I am going to write the story of my life?"

The long gray eyes, already wide with the joy of having

seen his own creation read, met mine with the expression of
mild satiety that an announcement of another undertaking
of this kind might be expected to bring to an author's eyes.
Yet it seems to me, in memory now, that I read his story
with the same slight prickling of the skin that — when I
was sixteen — accompanied my introduction to Zola's *Nana*.

"Is it a Halloween story, Mom-mom?"

"I hadn't thought of it that way. Do you think someone
— long ago — turned me into a bad little girl?"

"I don't know." Hans shrugged his shoulders and turned
his back, suggesting that he was impatient with me for
having asked a question that he was too young to answer.

Or was I the one, preferring presumption to humility in
conversation, who felt the impatience that suddenly ended
our talk? "I don't know either," I said. "And I wish I
knew — what happened to the little girl I used to be."

Of our four grandchildren, Hans most resembles Eric.
And looking into the freckled oval of Hans's flushed face,
I remembered a time when Eric, after listening to one of
my tearful accounts of a recent misunderstanding with his
father, said, "Mother, your life is a horror story. You should
be writing it, not telling it."

"I'll try," I said, feeling more pleased than I could say.
The word "horror," although sufficiently fustian to dry
my tears, was true enough to be taken seriously and, like
"Halloween," is reminiscent of the witchcraft, cruel spells,
and assorted terrors that parents, while denying the existence
of such powers, often use to enchant their children. These
contradictions in my own experience have so much of the
gaiety — and incongruity — of Halloween in them that it

is possible, now that I think of them, to smile at them, as one smiles into the hideously masked face of a child who, having rung the doorbell, trustingly extends both hands for a share of the Halloween plunder. In retrospect, certainly, my life becomes a time when the natural and the supernatural were indistinguishable and nobody thought it strange.

Certainly it never seemed to me either that I was overly credulous or my father more indolent than his contemporaries and, without the expressed judgment of others in respect to our behavior, I might not have known that my father and I were bewitched. Naturally, we did not speak of enchantment as a possibility, even though some of our neighbors had used a broom to counteract the power of my grandfather's "evil eye." Since my father seemed to think that his failures, like his good health, were expressions of God's love and immutable, I shared this belief. His cheerful manner showed, I thought, that this was true. His speech, in fact, seemed to vibrate with the authenticity of reminiscence so that, God willing, our return to the Garden of Eden would not have surprised me. The impression of his speech was such that, listening to it, I could see Adam — smiling — and Eve — unsmiling — while a shadowy figure, not unlike my father's, helped to tend the garden.

At the same time I seemed to share my father's disapproval of Eve and women generally, who were both as ambitious and serious as Eve had been. "Beware of mad dogs and cross women," he said. But of course mad dogs were a rarity and the kind of serious woman that, perhaps,

Eve was did not come into my life until my formal education began. As a child, I knew only the anger I was able
to provoke in Aunt Hester and my mother. This anger
flashed in the darkened summer sky and was gone — although I was a good deal shaken by it — and forgotten.
When my father said, "Beware of cross women," he meant
the kind of ill humor that keeps a person from smiling, the
deep discontent that brought Eve into an argument with
the serpent when she might have been smiling at one of
Adam's dissertations on the origin of species. In other
words, my father's definition of a cross woman included
all of those women who failed to smile when he addressed
them.

Always sympathetic with his sisters-in-law, my father
made exceptions of the unsmiling ones. At the same time,
he made excuses for them when I complained to him of
what seemed to me to have been a certain crossness.
"Hester had a dog's life," he said. "She was hired out to
the Grubbs when she was thirteen and the Grubbs showed
no mercy to their hired girls. Nobody was more greedy
than old Mose Grubb."

On the basis of these remarks, I tried to think of my Aunt
Hester as a true martyr. Her wedding picture shows a
lean young woman, wistful and already slightly wizened,
who looks as if — in the instant the camera's shutter
snapped — she foresaw her young husband's early death and
the forty years of drudgery that began with her widowhood.
Yet my father's sister Hester — although hired out at the
same age and widowed at fifty — appears plumply co-
quettish on her wedding picture. Both Aunt Hesters visited

our house during my mother's absences or illnesses, to make my life more agreeable than, without them, it might have been. The former scolded me in a martyred whine that depresses me, even now, and the latter applied her knuckles to the top of my head with a brisk efficiency that still impresses me. And painful though my father's sister's discipline was, I smile now when I think of it because her smile was so wide and warm not only on her wedding picture but whenever, during her widowhood, we stopped at her house. Subject to mild heart attacks and fits of temper, her smile then made her failures seem as unimportant as, in reality, they were. And so I accept my father's belief that a failure to smile is, for a woman, the final failure.

Then it follows that it was Eve's failure to smile when the serpent approached her that made their unfortunate dialogue, and Adam's loss of the Garden of Eden, inevitable. To this belief my father and I agreed when we walked in the fields where a constant breeze, presumably from those rivers that flowed to the east of Eden, seemed to be scented with odors of newly created things. At such times my father's manner implied a familiarity with the Garden of Eden that was equal to — if not greater than — Adam's and his voice vibrated so that, hearing it, I too seemed to *remember* Adam smiling and Eve unsmiling. And having shared that recollection of Adam, all smiles and affability, I suppose it was natural for me, my father's daughter, to have shared in his judgment of Eve and those women of our acquaintance who took a humorless view of life.

Along with his dread of cross women, therefore, I began my life with a sense of having visited the Garden of Eden.

It may be that with less credulity on my part, my life might have been better. But of course a better life would not have been my life. Our enjoined credulity amused us then and it still amuses me. I hope that amusement will make it possible for me to tell the story of my life in the spirit of Halloween.

ii

SCHOOL DAYS AND NIGHTS

ALL THAT I KNEW of the Belsnickels' visit was what my mother told me. "You seemed to be laughing, Belle. But when I lifted you out of the cradle, you were stiff."

Had she expected me to be as fearless as she was or, on my first Christmas Eve, to know that Belsnickels are a combination of Beelzebub and Saint Nicholas — patron saint of Russia, seafarers, virgins, and children — designed to scare the devil out of a child before they shower her with Christmas gifts and, knowing this, had she wrongly assumed that I, at the age of six months, was already willing to be separated from my naughtiness?

Certainly the disappointment and shock she suffered on account of my failure to have enjoyed the Belsnickels' visit seemed to have lined her face for life. My fear of masked faces, too, seems to be fixed in me.

The second night of learning — one that my mother never mentioned when we were older — was related to the appearance of Halley's comet. This does not mean that I saw the comet. Nor can I now be sure that my parents did. The premonition that our place, newly green and gay with the April song of birds and frogs, might be lost, had grown from a daily account of the comet's progress that my father read aloud from the newspaper.

Death was no stranger to me — happily. After four years of a mutually embarrassing senility, death had taken my grandmother from her cheerful bedroom to the cemetery. Birds caught by the cats were eaten head first by their captors. Hens now breeding their chicks in those coops that my mother was, at this very moment, draping in old carpet to discourage the predations of mink and weasel would, in the summer when their young no longer needed them, become the chicken in a lovely pot pie. Death followed life and, in our house, we shed few tears for the dead. So casually, indeed, did my parents appear to accept death that I — sleepless because my mother was critically ill and I was afraid to go on living without her — decided to be buried, in the event of her death, with her. Relieved, then, because this difficult decision had been made, I went to sleep unafraid.

The thought of a collision between the earth and Halley's

comet, however, was so unfamiliar that pure horror had
seized me that night while my mother moved among the
hen coops. Wordless, therefore, I began to scream.

"If you don't stop that," my mother said, "I'll whip you.
What will the neighbors think?"

It was, in slightly different form, the question I had
asked over and over while we waited for Halley's comet to
destroy us. But since my mother's way of asking it implied
reproof instead of the comfortable exchange of ideas that
I wanted to hear, I supposed that Halley's comet was no
more frightening to my mother than the Belsnickels had
been. And since that possibility, too, was unthinkable I ran
— wordless and sobbing — into the house, where my grandfather set me on his knees and held me there until my fear
of the world's end took on the watery aspect of a dream —
a terrible dream from which I awoke innumerable times in
the final years of my childhood to find that earth's place
remains pretty much the same.

The faith that my grandfather had shown when, wordless,
he set me on his knees eventually became mine and supported me in a series of efforts that, for want of a better
name, may be called "my school days." A fear for the
earth's survival, having become the third in a pantheon
of fears that began with false faces and included cross
women, inconvenienced me in every way that fear without
faith initially does and, perhaps, was necessary for my survival. Almost certainly, it was helpful to the degree it
curbed a natural exuberance that continued to be un-
affected by my mother's frequent repetition of "What will
the neighbors think?"

I did not understand her interest in our neighbors' minds,

or what appeared to be a constant anxiety lest my conduct displease them, since her own behavior indicated as little fear of what-will-the-neighbors-think? as it did of Belsnickels and Halley's comet. Yet it was apparent, on my first day of school, how much she wanted the neighbors to think well of me.

Even more than that, on the first September morning, when I trotted away in the direction of the schoolhouse, I felt her need to warn me of all the dangers a little girl might meet on a long, winding road to school. But there had been no time for warnings. Reuben, "a manly little boy" for whom my father expressed great admiration, must not be kept waiting even though my braids — unaccustomed to being decorated with bows of wide ribbon so early in the morning — had given my mother a good bit of trouble. So much trouble, really, that Reuben called on the telephone to say he would not wait for me. That he did wait on that first day of school attested, I suppose, to his manliness, a virtue that on the next day — or ever again — would not permit him to be as tardy as I often was. Recovered from the shock of learning from his father on the next day that Reuben had long since left for school, I ran through the woods alone and, in the years that followed, was surprised by nothing Reuben did.

"Grandpop will come to meet you after school," my mother had said when my braids were properly bound and decorated on my first day of school.

Fearful of dead trees and "tramps" — both to be found in the Elmira Furnace woods — I was not afraid to be alone by day. It was, in fact, my natural state and odd, I thought, that my mother was determined, on this day, to change it. "I don't want him to come to meet me," I said.

But it was plain in the way she smiled at me that her mind was set on having my grandfather meet me after school and, indeed, no sooner had Reuben, my guardian of the morning, gone into his house than my grandfather appeared on the crest of the hill where Mrs. Baker lived.

He was comfortably seated where the upper bar of the rail fence had been let down to allow passage from the road into a field. His dusty black slouch hat was draped over one knee while both hands rested on the handle of his cane and his straight white hair floated in the breeze. He was dignified, handsome, and the companion with whom I had survived the ordeal of Halley's comet and seen my first flicker. Yet now it was as though I, like Christopher Columbus on his return from the new world, had to be helped to find my own country. Angrily, because by this time our house was in plain view, I chided my grandfather for having done what my mother had asked him to do and ran home ahead of him. I did not know until many years later that all homecomings have, along with the jubilation, humiliation. Or we might say — with Columbus in mind — that all homecoming is, in a sense, a return in chains.

At any rate my first day in school was not the kind of tour de force that leads to freedom. My teacher's wide mustache and penetrating glance were remarkably like the "Minuit look" shared by my father and grandfather. The picture of George Washington crossing the Delaware that hung behind the teacher's desk was reminiscent of my grandfather's calm on the April evening when Halley's comet frightened me out of my wits. Homelike, too, was the way the clock's big black hands visibly moved toward the times for recess, dinner, and our dismissal at half past three in the afternoon.

Looking up at my grandmother's clock on the kitchen shelf fifty years later, Eric said, "That clock knows everything." And now, when I think of the schoolhouse clock, it seems as though it, too, knew everything. Surely it knew that "a word fitly spoken is like apples of gold in pictures of silver."

A disciple of Daniel Webster himself, my father lived by this proverb and, on a Sunday morning after I had interjected a careless line into a dialogue he was sharing with my mother, spanked me for what he considered a failure on my part to speak fitly. On another Sunday, when my mother and I were walking home from the church service with Aunt Hester, my father's sister, I was moved to interrupt their conversation with a speech of incoherent obscenities that moved Aunt Hester to say, "That child, if she lives, will be a disgrace to our whole family." She spoke with so much assurance that my mother and I, without having previously considered that possibility, thereafter considered it and said little — obscene or decorous — to Aunt Hester. Nor do I recall that my mother, Aunt Hester, and I ever again walked home from a church service together. Yet, in retrospect, it seems that knowing the importance of "a word fitly spoken" has eased for me the malaise of living and learning.

After a short time of experimentation with the epic form

— an original effort that relieved my exuberant need for expression and bored the little girl who now listened while we walked home from church — I discovered the poetry in my school reader and began to recite it both at home and in school. Robert Browning's "Incident of the French Camp" came to me early and stayed in my affections — if not my memory — until this writing:

> You know, we French stormed Ratisbon:
>   A mile or so away,
> On a little mound, Napoleon
>   Stood on our storming-day;
> With neck out-thrust, you fancy how,
>   Legs wide, arms locked behind,
> As if to balance the prone brow
>   Oppressive with its mind.
>
> Just as perhaps he mused "My plans
>   That soar, to earth may fall,
> Let once my army-leader Lannes
>   Waver at yonder wall," —
> Out 'twixt the battery-smokes there flew
>   A rider, bound on bound
> Full-galloping; nor bridle drew
>   Until he reached the mound.
>
> Then off there flung in smiling joy,
>   And held himself erect
> By just his horse's mane, a boy:
>   You hardly could suspect —
> (So tight he kept his lips compressed,
>   Scarce any blood came through)
> You looked twice ere you saw his breast
>   Was all but shot in two.

"Well," cried he, "Emperor, by God's grace
    We've got you Ratisbon!
The Marshal's in the market-place,
    And you'll be there anon
To see your flag-bird flap his vans
    Where I, to heart's desire,
Perched him!" The chief's eye flashed; his plans
    Soared up again like fire.

The chief's eye flashed; but presently
    Softened itself, as sheathes
A film the mother-eagle's eye
    When her bruised eaglet breathes;
"You're wounded!" "Nay," the soldier's pride
    Touched to the quick, he said:
"I'm killed, Sire!" And his chief beside,
    Smiling the boy fell dead.

My father had not heard Aunt Hester predict a disgraceful ending to my speaking career and I doubt that he
would have been much affected in any event. When it was
time for us to entertain at the school's spring package party,
he stayed at home and one of the men — who had never
seen my mother in her blue serge dress (the skirt of which
was so truly "a hobble skirt" that, on one shopping trip,
she was thrown to the pavement when she stepped
from the street to the curb) — said, "Who's the good-
looking girl?" My mother was greatly pleased and so was I.
She was pleased, too, by my recitation of "The Raggedy
Man" and I felt sure that the words of James Whitcomb
Riley's poem were "like apples of gold in pictures of silver."
It was this success and my mother's smiling acceptance of
it that must have prompted me to recite "The Raven" two
years later.

By that time Aunt Hester's harsh judgment of me and her habit of drumming on the top of my outsized head with her knuckles had been replaced by a dignified silence in which she was willing, it seemed, to be shown that I might — all signs to the contrary — yet become a source of joy and comfort to our family. Sympathetically my father had explained to me that Aunt Hester's way of using her knuckles — since she was childless — could be expected to be somewhat crude. He recalled having had an uncle whose skill in "knuckling" was the result of daily practice on three available heads — his own, my Aunt Anna's, and Aunt Hester's. It was the accepted way of quieting small children when they were small children. Afterwards, he spoke more precisely of Aunt Hester and said, "Let me tell you, Belle, where she can't be boss, there's trouble." And I smiled, thinking how very true that had been when I was a small child in her care on the days my mother went to sell eggs in town.

So, in an attempt to calm Aunt Hester's uneasiness and my own, I recited "The Raven." And when the last "nevermore" had been said, my father who, from time to time, urged me to "exercise my memory" in the hope of its becoming as cogent as his own applauded with downcast eyes. Later, when I asked her how she liked my recital, my mother said, "It was too much to learn at once, Belle. I'd say a shorter piece next time."

But the momentum of the exercise that had won my father's approval and eventually would convince Aunt Hester of my worth to the whole family was so much greater than my appreciation of my mother's advice that my next recitation was longer, not shorter, than "The Raven." I noticed that the girls, whose fathers had not encouraged them to exercise their memories, now walked behind me on the road from the church to our homes on Sunday afternoons and held up their hands, when I turned to look at them, to hide the awful width of their smiles. Yet it never occurred to me that I should "say a shorter piece next time." It was four years later, when I was twelve years old, that my first lapse of memory — in the middle of a long recital in the middle of the Sunday school's Christmas program — put an end to my memorable feats of memory. My mother said, "It wouldn't have been noticed if you had known enough to sit down."

But of course I had noticed the sudden lack of words in the air and knew that somehow my contribution to the Christmas entertainment had turned into "a disgrace to the whole family." It was too soon to guess that I would never again recite "The Raven" verbatim.

And in retrospect it seems, as Eric once said of the grandmother's clock in our kitchen, that the memory I exercised then was not mine at all but rather a gift I borrowed from a big black-handed clock that knew "everything." Now all of my favorite memory gems — "Lord Ullin's Daughter," "Sir Galahad," "The Destruction of Sennacherib," "Lochinvar's Ride," and even "Abou Ben Adhem," a hero who was not really a favorite of mine — have been forgotten. I will not repeat any of them for my grandchildren when I am eighty — as my father recited "The Boys" on his eightieth birthday anniversary for Eric.

All is forgotten — sadly and incredibly — excepting the way we used to walk home in a rain of yellow birch leaves and touch the purple arrowwood while chipmunks and chewinks rustled where the acorns fell. I remember, too, how fervently we prayed — after Halley's comet — that our quiet world would never end. And recently, after Reuben's funeral, Raymond reminded me of something more.

My relationship with Reuben had been more casual than close from the beginning. Of necessity we traveled the same road to and from the schoolhouse. After Reuben's refusal to wait for me on the second day, however, I went to school alone and returned home in the evening with Reuben and the teacher and those other pupils who lived close by. After we had turned into the road where Reuben and I lived, he often spoke of the things "a manly little boy" might be expected to know and I listened with a non-committing silence that, almost certainly, would have discouraged a less confident informer. Quite unexpectedly one afternoon, he challenged me to a wrestling match that —when I was on the verge of winning—his father stopped. Whether the interruption was intended to save my honor or Reuben's, I could not tell.

Nor can I say with certainty how many years passed before Reuben's second challenge occurred. All I know now is that it followed on the heels of his unsuccessful *passage d'armes* with a boy who was, I thought, more agreeable than Reuben, and came as a great surprise to me — a surprise that involved, with the exception of our teacher, the whole school population and indicated, almost certainly, a demoniac tendency in Reuben. How truly demoniac Reuben's plan really was became plain to me when, on the day of his funeral, Raymond's wife said, "Did you know that Reuben and Raymond had a fight over you and Raymond won?"

"No, I didn't know that," I said. "But I knew that Reuben was mad at me." And since at that time I never associated Reuben's sometimes challenging behavior with my preference for another, it seemed unnecessary to do so now — even though the question Raymond's wife had asked me did, in a way, explain all of Reuben's madness.

So that for the first time in many years I remembered a certain "madness" that had taken hold of Reuben during one noontime while we were pretending to be mules hitched to a load of charcoal in the woods. The mule team included a majority of the pupils and excluded Reuben who — on account of his "manliness" — was the teamster. And certainly there was no one in the school who could have shouted, "Gee, haw, get up, and whoa" with the authority that Reuben's voice carried. When he shouted, "Whoa" on the day of his madness, we stopped our prancing and waited, naturally, for further directions.

What happened then, however, was not natural. The two big boys who regularly served as "wheel" mules, without an audible command from Reuben, had stopped being mules and pinioned both of my arms while Reuben approached me from the front.

There he prodded my thighs with a stick and commanded me to remove — forgetting that my hands were not free — the undergarment that was, in fact, under two petticoats and a dress that reached below my knees. Raymond, forewarned of Reuben's overweening desire to see that superior manliness — indicated by Raymond's victory in man-to-man combat — publicly proven by rape, had disappeared into the woods and stayed until one of the wheel mules said, "Let her go."

Since the teacher did not seem to have heard my cries, I assume that the ringing of the school bell immediately thereafter was one of those fortuitous happenings for which I am most grateful. In any event, with the ringing of the school bell, everyone excepting Reuben became a mule again and Raymond, looking relieved and agreeable as ever, emerged from the woods.

Now, having seen Reuben surrounded by both flowers and mourners, Raymond looks at me and says, "Oh my. Oh my."

The curiosity I feel is natural in the presence of a love we lost more than fifty years ago. I smile to let Raymond who, it seems, is a sensitive man know that I understand his inability to think of anything else to say. It was, perhaps, the best of all possible ways to show how relieved, at last, he was.

iii

A TIME OF TRIBULATION

My INITIAL APPEARANCE must have seemed to my parents
— who had been comely children — a genetical joke of the
worst kind. Yet to that disappointment (since my father,
almost certainly, expected to have a beautiful daughter and
my mother a handsome son) a neighborly Hathor had
added the prophetic weight of her own discontent by saying,
"This child will never be right." And although my father
was not equally aware of my oddity, since I resembled him,
he seemed to remember my birth as the first of a series of

events that he later, with a broad smile, referred to as "a time of great tribulation."

At other times, recalling one of the many discomforts he had survived, he said, "Belle, you don't know what a panic is."

My father never smiled when he spoke of "a panic." And, now that I think of it, neither did I. A panic was a tribulation of the worst kind and too familiar to be funny.

By the time I was thirteen, indeed, this condition was as familiar as my own reflection in a mirror. Unable to do anything else, I had accepted both with cheerfulness. Without panic, perhaps, I might have been one of those stillborn babies whose sad little tombstones (mixed with the massive markers of the old) often brought my churchyard walks to a pensive pause. Before one of those nameless markers I am, even now, reborn. My mother has told me how it was.

"In the beginning there was no pain," she said. "Panic" does not occur to her as often as it does to my father. "When the doctor came, he gave me something to start the pain. And then there was pain."

What she felt on the June night when I was born was pain — not panic. Yet the look of panic is in her wide brown eyes and I believe that Pan was present; so that she never again could share my father's interest in ordinary people and, as a consequence, thought that the baby born to her was more unusual than babies usually are. Her suggestion that I should be named Helen, I think, is indicative of her initial reaction to the fact that she had survived the night's pain. She said, however, that she had wanted to

give me that name because of my resemblance to a favorite
cousin of my father's whose name was Helen Minuit. So
it was my father who — whether moved by bravado or love,
I do not know — called me Belle and gave me, in my name,
a talisman that is, at least, as useful as Cain's God-given
"mark." It is very difficult, certainly, for me to imagine living my life by any other name. Hearing it now, I still
feel the depths of my parents' concern for me and know how
great their forbearance was when they agreed to call me
Belle.

Nor does it seem to me, in retrospect, that their feelings
were affected by the knowledge that among their acquaintances there was one who said, "That child will never be
right." Webster's dictionary considers the meaning of
"right" (Old English *riht*) at such length, giving so much
variety to its application, that my father who resorted to
the dictionary frequently may have said of "right," as he
often said of beauty, "It's a matter of opinion." Whatever
his own opinion was — either on my chances of becoming
"right" or the frank denial of them by one of his acquaintances — my father had kept it to himself. My mother,
repeating the grim prophecy to me a few years later, had
looked as gaily scornful as a Gypsy fortune-teller might have
looked while listening to the inept fortune-telling of a
Gaji rival. And she never told me who it was who, looking
into the family cradle, had spoken so unkindly of her
child.

The words, however, have a familiar flavor. They are so
like another pronouncement that was made in my presence
one Sunday when my mother and Aunt Hester and I were

walking home from church. "That child, if she lives long enough, will be a disgrace to the whole family." Both predictions are in keeping with her disposition to use words (knowing how futile, in my case, knuckling had been) instead of the sticks and stones commonly used by persons of contradictory beliefs to reduce their opponents to a quiescent state. That my state on the walk from church had not been quiescent and that Aunt Hester and my mother had certain differences of opinion go without saying. Both were fond of my father. In other respects, ideally, they stood as far apart as their physical proximity would allow.

Sometimes Aunt Hester continued her dialogues with my father behind the barn in what my mother considered a shocking display of bad manners. My own observation was that Aunt Hester seldom arrived at our house in a good humor and, having perchance come with a smile, usually left in a huff. All in all, Aunt Hester was inclined to be waspish while her sister, my Aunt Anna, poured oil on the troubled waters that had risen as I grew older, around my mother. Time in short, had been unkind to both of my Aunt Hesters.

My father occasionally elaborated on this theme by saying, "Anna stood a much better chance with the boys." Yet their photographs showed them to have been so like one another that it was difficult for me to tell the one from the other; and my mother, irritated by one of my attacks of independence, had so often said, "You're just like Aunt Hester" that I spent many an idle moment in an attempt to see why the boys had preferred Aunt Anna. The pictures, in reality, gave Aunt Hester the greater vitality and presence before the camera. Both, as my father averred, were petite and quite pretty. Yet Aunt Anna had married at the age of eighteen and Aunt Hester in her thirty-fifth year. It was during the years of waiting for Aunt Hester's marriage that my father, who was not married until his thirty-fourth year, presumably formed the habit of saying, "Where Hester can't be the boss, there's trouble."

Afterwards he did not smile. The trouble with Aunt Hester had been more serious, it seemed, than the difficult decade he remembered as "a time of tribulation." The *tribulum*, if it touched my father at all, had touched him as lightly as Aunt Hester's trouble did.

It was my mother, I thought, who knew how it feels to have the wheat of one's soul separated from its chaff. It was my mother, with her cryptic insight into the heart of a person and her will to love that person nonetheless, who had suffered the blows of the flail. It was to my mother that Aunt Hester had said, "That child, if she lives long enough, will be a disgrace to the whole family." "That child" was my mother's.

Death, having threatened her in three illnesses, had turned away from my mother and seized other members of her family in succession, until there was a death for each of the years I remember as "childhood." Yet when I was no longer a child and my father put his arm around my mother's lean waist and, smiling broadly at me, said, "We've come up out of great tribulation," I could not help smiling because, after all, it was my mother upon whom the flail seemed to have fallen while death came to my grandmother, both of my grandfathers, Aunt Hester's old husband, two of my mother's sisters-in-law, the hired man, a brother and a brother-in-law who were not nearly as old as Aunt Hester's husband, and a young nephew while my father, without an effort, withdrew into the kingdom of his own mind. And seeing how easy it was for my father to escape from the scene of "tribulation," I envied him with all of a heart divided between my wish to escape and a failure to do so.

This is not to say that I, at that time, either believed my father was "a baby" or that I "never looked like a baby" or that my mother was mistaken when she told me that this, alas, was the truth. These were half-truths discovered by a person in pain.

Nor, certainly, did I share my father's view of himself as "a gem," or flower wasted on the desert air, both immobile and unseen by anyone. I saw him and envied him because of his seemingly effortless escapes — there is no other word — from the circumstances that had broken my mother's health and spirit. It was as though, when my mother hitched her big sorrel mare to the phaeton and my father's legs were swathed in the white and yellow plaid horse blanket, I could see the young man who had survived the lightning's thrust at the Plow Hotel. In the interim his black hair has turned gray. But he is very much alive and, as the phaeton begins to move, I see him glare in all directions as though he thought my mother and I might, at the last moment, prevent his going. Yet we never did. The very idea was untenable, my envy notwithstanding.

Without my father's diary, I might not be able to recall exactly how and when that troubled time of our lives came to an end. Curiously enough it ended with a threshing season. On August 31, 1914, my father wrote, "Partly cloudy. Commenced to thresh grain. Threshed 413 bushels of oats." The next day was "Clear and warm. Finished threshing wheat. 178 bushels." On September 2, 1914, the diary says, "Clear and windy. About home all day. Father died at 8:30 o'clock this morning."

Although the sight of the thresher's steam engine puffing cheerfully on the barn's earthen ramp and the voices of the neighbors who helped to thresh must have been as interesting as ever, I remember only the sound of my grandfather's hoarse breathing in the warm night after the threshing was finished.

The next September, when the threshing was done, I went to the normal school instead of the school in the Elmira Furnace woods. "I want you to be somebody," my mother said.

A Minuit and my father's only child, it was impossible for me to believe that I was not, in reality, *somebody.* There was nobody else that I wanted to be and my mother's wish to have me become somebody else was one that I could not gratify in any event. It was sufficiently tedious, I thought, to be leaving the familiar farm for an "education." "I wonder what Grandpop would say," I said.

His sympathy for my mother would have been too strong to let him speak on my behalf. She had lost weight as the day for my departure approached and now, standing at the door of my grandmother's bakehouse, her high forehead was so deeply lined and her cheeks so sunken it seemed to me that another illness threatened my mother. Yet my grandfather's presence, I thought, might have comforted both of us. Although I was eleven years old now and too big to sit on his knees, I wanted to tell him that I was going away to the normal school because my parents imagined that whatever was wrong with me would be removed by my enrollment there. It seems now that my father — since I resembled him more than I did my mother — was not equally aware of my oddity. In any event, it was my mother who said, "Belle, I want you to be somebody. And if you don't go to school now, you never will."

That my grandfather would have been proud of my courage in the face of my enrollment at the normal school, I was certain. But it would have been comforting to hear him say it.

Understandably tired of listening to my long recitations, the teacher had said, "Belle is ready to go to high school."

"But how? She can't run to and from Cooperstown," my parents said.

The possibility of my doing so had interested them, however, so that when a neighbor said, "She doesn't have to. You can find a boarding place for her in Cooperstown," they looked annoyed.

"That won't be necessary," I said. "They can buy me a horse and I will ride to Cooperstown." If Thomas Jefferson, as our American history text implied, had started the Democratic Party by riding a horse to the White House, there was no telling what might come of my riding one to and from high school. In any event the prospect of going to school on a real horse — after five years of pretending to be one — seemed too good to be true. "Please. Please. Please."

To this my mother, with one of the melancholy insights that must have been as irksome to her as they were to me, replied, "No. Something might happen. In the woods."

Born in the woods and, until now, schooled there, it was, in fact, the one place where I felt at ease. "My horse will not let anything happen," I said with feeling.

Unafraid in the woods himself, my father, at this point, frowned as though an idea more alarming than all the risks of woodland travel put together had occurred to him. "It's a three-year high school," he said.

"Then I'll graduate in three years," I said, seeing myself already returned to the woods and free as an Indian.

"But you won't be ready for college."

"College?"

"Belle, the time is here when everybody must go to college." His eyes avoided mine but his voice was so solemn that the shocking words could not be argued. Everyone smiled encouragingly at me then and, without further ado, agreed that, since this was so, I might as well be enrolled in the normal school without delay. "She'll be taken *care* of there," my father said, as though speaking to himself.

Beyond an occasional nightmare, after eating too freely of pork sausage, and my annual attack of green apple colic, I had felt no need of care. It was interesting, I thought, to hear the word in connection with my parents' decision to send me to that state-endowed school from which my father had graduated. Subsequent conversation with my parents had failed to convince me that what I mistakenly felt to be my need for a horse was, in reality, a need for further instruction. Certainly I felt no need for *care* on the day of our interview with the normal school's principal and, if asked what I thought I most needed that day in the middle of May, I would have said: "a horse." This need, indeed, seemed to have increased while the phaeton moved along in the red dust behind my mother's sorrel thoroughbred and the farm disappeared behind the long line of cedars that bordered our neighbor's field. Mercifully, the phaeton carried us along in blissful ignorance of the future, so that our leisurely progress was pleasant.

"You'll never regret going to school, Belle. An education is the one thing that nobody can take from you," my father said.

More than these conciliatory remarks — interesting though they were in the face of my silent composure — needed to be said. I try to imagine now what might have been said if we could have known on that bright May day that more than fifty years would pass before my need for a horse of my own could be met. I wonder, too, what my parents' feelings would be if they knew that, after fifty years, I am too old to enjoy riding. But the silence, that on that day was mine alone, is now complete.

Since my father and the principal had met when both were students in the normal school, our interview got off to a good start. The principal was a tall man who, in spite of being several years younger than my father, looked more sad and sallow than my father or, indeed, anyone I had ever seen. And when he gazed over his gold-rimmed glasses at me one of the small muscles near the corner of his mouth twitched — the way the skin of a horse might twitch to dislodge a fly. "How old is she?"

"Ten," my mother said, looking pink and proud.

"But she's only a child," the principal said, pinching the corners of his loose-lipped mouth together. "She needs a mother's care."

This probably was one of the last things my mother expected to hear. "But she's big enough to take care of herself and will be eleven next month." Both the sound of her voice and the color of her cheeks showed how surprised she was to find that she had traveled thirty miles to hear an opinion contrary to her own.

At this point my father easily could have said, "Belle is a big girl, Lucy. But she doesn't take care of herself." And it may be that he, who so often said, "Honesty is the best policy," was ready to tell the principal that my mother always braided my hair and washed behind my ears when the silence was broken by a black-bearded man who put his right hand on the top of my head — instead of offering it to anyone — and said, "She has a good head. We'll take her."

My mother smiled then and so did everyone who was there, excepting the principal. When the interview was over and we were at home again, she said, "What else could we do?"

No one ever answered my mother's question. Seeing how pale and thin she was when the threshing was done that summer, I had stopped saying, "I wonder what Grandpop would say."

We remembered the old friend of Aunt Hester's who said, "It is a mistake to send Belle away — at her age. I knew a girl who went to college too soon and she wasn't *well.* Later."

Whether his association with Aunt Hester, or the similarity between his foreboding and hers, had prejudiced my mother the fact was that she did not let his advice move her. "But Belle is a big girl. And looks much older than ten. We're not going to listen to that man."

Privately I fancied that her determination to send me to the normal school was related to her tendency to see my father as a "baby" and me as a woman who, oddly enough, never had been anything else. It was a way of looking at us that favored my father in many ways — as though perennial youth were not enough — and robbed me of the gift that properly belonged to me. And, in retrospect, my resentment seems quite natural.

Yet it was my mother's inability to see me as a child that made it possible for me to forget that I was one. And even if I had foreseen that in the next four years I would lose both my childhood and the memory that had made it possible for me to recite "The Raven" verbatim, I would have remained, uncomplainingly, at the normal school because she said, "You must stay there, Belle. The neighbors will laugh at me if you come home." Certainly it was unthinkable that I — aware of the laughter her disdain for the ordinary, in combination with my own eccentricities, occasionally caused — should, by anything as conventional as failure to graduate from the normal school, provoke the neighbors to laugh at my mother.

Then, perhaps, my father had thought me too young to appreciate the advice he gave me thirty years later. "Belle, you must be patient with her. Your mother has been very sick." Nor was it necessary to remind me of her three illnesses — then. Hearsay and observation had etched them on the windows of my mind so that they, like a frieze of frost on glass, subdued the light by which otherwise I might have seen myself and others more clearly. For example, I am surprised now to read in my father's diary under the date of June 11, 1915, "I was sick. About home all day." And since there is no record of a visit by the doctor until the day before "Lucy came home from the normal school," there is no way of knowing how severe my father's sickness was, or its cause. The distraught quality, with many erasures, of his handwriting, points to a psychosomatic stress connected with my departure. This is only a guess of the sort that a person standing in a warm house and looking at a frost-covered window can make about the stranger at the door.

Finally, on Monday, September 20, we read, "Clear and warm. Lucy came home from the normal school." This sentence is followed by a list of expenses and the words "Harrowed seeding ground." It was not necessary, it seems, to have mentioned the fact that I was — at last — in the *care* of the normal school.

Without my father's diary I could not tell when my mother finally left me at the normal school in the care of my cousin Edwina and the school's faculty. My poor memory needs no help to recall the names and faces of the three girls who shared my room at various times during the next four years. Edwina, by this time, had gone to stay with another cousin who needed her and, for the first time in my life, the sight of food depressed me. Or was it the prospect of sharing a breakfast (after eating at the small table in the kitchen alone while my parents harnessed the mules at the barn) and the clatter of dishes in the big dining room that had taken away my appetite and left my throat too dry for speech or swallowing? This sense of desolation in the presence of a bowl of cold oatmeal and hundreds of young adults, was, I gradually realized, an uncomplicated case of homesickness that soon would give way to a complicated insomnia due to pipes on the wall of my room and an elementary algebra book.

Before leaving, Edwina advised me to put the algebra book under my pillow and sleep on it. "It is a very old prescription and can do no harm," she said with a bright smile.

"All right," I said. "I will do that."

Anything that would postpone the day when my failure to understand that algebra text proved me to be "a disgrace to our whole family," I thought, was worth trying. It was an interesting use of magic, moreover, and much less humiliating than a confession of my ignorance to the algebra teacher. And so — already willing to forget that "honesty is the best policy" — I took Edwina's advice. But of course she could not have known that I would not be able to "sleep on the book." It was the awful darkness, to which I was not accustomed on account of the lamp that always burned in my bedroom at home, in combination with the night noises of the steam pipes that, by keeping me awake, had rendered

Edwina's magic ineffective. Its use, however, was *my* mistake, the first of many.

Happily none of the others come to mind at this moment. In their stead I remember the reassuring, but distant, crowing of the roosters on those early mornings when homesickness had made my throat ache. I remember other things of slight consequence: the delicate white blossoms of the bloodroot that grew along the edges of the fields near the school and the excitement of finding a purple crocus there; the rain of warblers that came in the spring to feed on the larches budding outside the window where, supposedly, I was practicing on the piano; the boxes of apples my parents sent to me.

I remember my dresses, first spectacularly new — and odd because my mother thought that, being "odd," I should wear odd clothes — and later either outgrown or soiled enough to have inspired a classmate, on seeing that I was about to pay her a friendly visit, to shout, "Go-home-you-dirty-pig."

Now, with a slight effort, I can recall the names and faces of the three girls who were my roommates and the three misunderstandings we had. My first roommate was only slightly older than I was and we separated, at the suggestion of her father, at the end of our second year together. In retrospect the misunderstanding had nothing to do with either my oddity or the fact that I frequently wore my white middy blouses until their fronts were gray. It had something to do with her vow, at the age of twelve, to celibacy and my decision to find, among the boisterous boys who serenaded our window during study hours, a husband. Our separation was a great shock to me, naturally.

My second roommate was, like myself, an only child. Our separation followed a misunderstanding having to do with our material possessions. I had spilled ink on her tablecloth and, to even the score, she had appropriated my new nightgown. After which I had asked the preceptress for another room and returned alone to the room where Edwina had left me two years earlier. The only differences were that I was bigger, and had five failures, instead of one, to consider: algebra, plane geometry, solid geometry, and two roommates. What was worse than this — disgraceful to my whole family though it undoubtedly was — I had not learned to sleep alone in the dark with the chuckling steam pipes.

Awake, I prowled the wide dark halls at night and, wherever a door opened to my knock, begged a night's sleep. Most often it was my first roommate who took me in. And when spring came, I gathered a bouquet of white violets and bluets for the preceptress who, it seems, always slept very soundly. My gift of spring flowers, given without commenting on the sense of guilt I felt — since moving from one's own room to another after ten at night was strictly forbidden — seemed to surprise her, in any event, as much as it surprises me now to think of it.

My third roommate was approximately twice my age and our misunderstanding had to do with the disappearance of a small gold pin that was hers and that I, with her permission, had worn. After what was for me an oddly uncomfortable absence, the pin reappeared on her dresser and I did not wear it again. In comparison with the misunderstandings that had led to my lonely year with the noisy steam pipes, it was a minor misunderstanding.

On our graduation day, my third roommate took a picture of me, with my parents, on the playground where during the previous four years I had spent a good bit of time — alone — on the swings and sliding board. In this snapshot, my parents and I are equally tall and I am wearing the vacuous grin peculiar to prosperous young women in the years immediately after World War I. My father, deeply tanned from working in the fields, smiles. But my mother, who is an even darker shade of brown, had driven to the exercises in a new green touring car and seems, as the camera clicked, to have foreseen the difficulty she was bound to have with flat tires.

I am not dressed in green. My dress is blue and beautifully overgrown with large henna roses. Nor am I wearing a medieval "devil's bonnet" to signify that I have made a pact with the devil. Yet, quite plainly, both the beauty and pride of Satan spark my glance and the most indifferent student of Jules Michelet (*Satanism and Witchcraft*) can see that I am "possessed." And as though this snapshot were not sufficient proof of my condition, I remember my school clothes all suddenly outgrown and tossed into my trunk because, lacking all other signs of her disgrace, the possessed woman *grows*. The dark woman to my left, it seems, has known from the night of my birth that this would happen. What she does not know and perhaps may not guess is that it happened after a time of great tribulation — a time that began after she and Edwina had gone home. To mark the time more exactly, it began with a visit from the ten-year-old daughter of a woman whose official title was "The Matron." I still remember how beautiful the little girl was and how unexpectedly — in the middle of what I had hoped would be a polite call — she lifted the hem of my nightgown and peered underneath it. Presumably, since she did not visit me again, her mother had sent her to see whether or not I was *comme les autres*.

_iv_

HINDSIGHT AND FORESIGHT

ALTHOUGH MY MOTHER never said in so many words that
a witch had been present when I was born, she had, on
several occasions, found time to say, "You didn't look like
a baby, Belle. You weighed more than fourteen pounds."

"I did?" I laughed, thinking how nice it was for me to
have been big when, just as easily, I might have been small.

"Yes. More. I know it was more, because you were full
of water when you were born and you had lost some of it
before we weighed you. And when you were weighed you
still weighed fourteen pounds."

My experience by then was sufficient to allow me to imagine the reluctance that both my father and the doctor must have felt when, seeing that I was too big to be weighed on the butter scales, they thought of bringing the chicken scales from the barn. They decided that it wasn't necessary. It was at this point, I guessed, that the doctor had climbed into the cherry tree and breakfasted on Black Tartarians. Since my mother's account of her accouchement reported this but left my father's actions unaccounted for, I supposed that he, having given me one look and marked the date in his diary, had taken long steps in the direction of the Plow Hotel. So it was my mother who brought the beam scales to the house a few days later and, with the help of a woman of the neighborhood, looped my ankles together and, while I hung from the scales like a fat rooster, weighed me.

Pleasant as this mental picture of my mother's strength and my size was, it seemed to me then — as, indeed, it still does — that if as my mother's facial expression implied, I was the biggest baby ever born, the doctor's failure to weigh me was a very unfortunate oversight.

"You weren't really a *baby*, you know," my mother said. "Your hair wasn't like a baby's hair. It was nearly *black*. And *heavy*."

"Like Pop's hair when he was young?" The Samsonian splendor of my father's hair, which on account of its premature graying I had never seen, was a family legend and the only thing of which as a family we dared to be proud without fear of the "fall" that invariably results from having "a haughty spirit."

"Yes, a little like his hair," my mother said.

At this, while the sun warmed the patch of rainbow-striped carpet where I was sitting with my father's copy of Wood's *Natural History* open to a black and white illustration of the kudu, delight expanded, like a huge flower, inside my rib cage. "What else happened when I was born?"

"They said you'd never be right."

"Somebody said that?" Surely, I thought, nobody looking into the pine cradle that had rocked my father and now held me could have said such a thing. Nobody we knew could have been so unkind.

"Yes." And instead of laughing, as I had hoped she would in order to show me that she took this prophecy no more seriously than she might have taken any foolish expression of humor or spite, my mother then set her foot on the sewing machine treadle and began to sew.

If there were one thing that I wish I had never known, it would be the magic of that moment. For, having repeated the spell and neglected to name the one who first made it, my mother made the words her own and, because of another incident of a similar kind, doubly effective. On that occasion, too, my mother was sewing. But we were not alone. An older woman, whose name is forgotten, was present. This woman smiles and waits for my mother to answer a question that I, distracted by the fall of the bridge I was attempting to build with my blocks, have not understood. There is a foxiness in the woman's smile, however, that makes me hold my breath until my mother says, "No. I'd rather sew for a boy. They have cuter clothes."

At this point, all of the small sounds of the house stop. My grandmother's clock on the kitchen shelf and the chunks of chestnut wood burning in the big stove are still. It is almost as though the world had ended when, with red cheeks and bright eyes, my mother threaded the basting needle and cut the thread with her teeth. My father is absent, having gone to buy woodland to be turned into charcoal or, perhaps to the Plow Hotel to escape from the sound of the sewing machine. Years later, he said, "I wanted you to be a girl." And certainly I have no reason to doubt it. Having made this declaration of affection, however, my father closed his eyes, as though the sight of me, a full-grown woman — when to have been his only child and a solitary blossom on the dying family tree should have been quite enough — had depressed him more than he could say. For whenever he spoke of women the pitch of his voice rose and his eyebrows met in a startled frown. So seldom in fact, did the women we knew meet with his wholehearted approval that I can think of only three: my mother's mother; Aunt Anna, my father's sister; and my mother. These — the first for her innumerable feats of strength in the management of her household and ten children, the second for a tact so exquisite that it bordered on the angelic, and my own mother for the remarkable tenacity that had made her marriage with my father endure for almost sixty years — these were the lovable exceptions who had proved to my father how right his wariness of women was. His indulgence of me was an outgrowth of his conviction, frequently mentioned, that "in the eyes of a parent, the child is always a child."

Somewhat sheepishly, therefore, I became a woman, and soon afterward met George Adams, who, like myself, had been sent by his parents to be a student at Red Rock College.

There, seeing that I hesitated at the entrance to the classroom where freshman registration was in progress, George turned to me and said, "I'm George Adams. Who are you?"

George resembled a picture often used to illustrate the story of Beauty and the Beast. And though nothing in his manner suggested that he wished to be disenchanted, I smiled at him and answered his question as politely as Beauty herself might have done. At nineteen, he was five inches taller than my father, and *like* him. Their likeness showed in George's heavy-lipped smile and in the way his eyes, after one quick glance at me, had focused on something beyond the top of my head. Most of all, it showed in the quick forward movement — a kind of leap, really — that could fill the heart of a child with awe. Noticing that the heavy soles of George's brown boots were covered by a film of dried mud, I wanted to ask him where he had left his plow, with its team of mules standing untended, while he walked to Red Rock. It seemed to me that I saw in his face the surprised look country people wear when they find themselves in the city. But I had time to say, "I'm Belle Minuit" — nothing more. The next moment, George was smiling at the brown-eyed blonde who stood beside me and saying, "I'm George Adams. Who are you?"

Remembering then how often my mother had said, "Smile, Belle; you will scare the boys if you look like that," I smiled again.

After the evening meal, when the first-year girls were together in the music room of the dormitory to which Emmeline and I had been assigned and we began to give our reasons for having registered at Red Rock College, I said, "I've come to get a husband."

Everyone laughed at this — everyone, that is, but me, for with six cousins, all older and prettier than myself, still single, I realized that the getting of a husband was a serious undertaking. My parents, moreover, had complicated matters by suggesting that I marry someone "of my own kind."

"By the way," one of the older girls said, "are you related to George Adams?"

"No. Why do you ask?"

"You look like him — like you might be his sister."

I said, "I think he looks a little like my father."

"That's very interesting."

"Not to me. I'm looking for a husband who is *not* like my father. My father and I look alike, too. And I'm afraid of him."

"She'll get over that," the girl in charge of the orientation meeting said. "Won't she, Emmeline?"

Emmeline was three years older than I. Her forehead was, like the nun's in Chaucer's prologue to *The Canterbury Tales*, almost a span broad. More, it was high enough to support a set of whimsical bangs that I would have given my premature wisdom tooth to possess. And she looked across the room at me then with what may well have been a calm acceptance of her own superiority. "Everybody likes George Adams," she said. "He comes of a good family. But of course you've heard of the Adamses."

"No. Unless you mean the President Adamses."

"Don't worry about it," she said. "It isn't *that* important."

The next time George and I met, he was Emmeline's
date and I was with an upperclassman who, like George,
enjoyed a considerable popularity. The occasion was a serious lecture by the Rabbi Stephen Samuel Wise. There
is no explanation, therefore, for the fact that in the middle
of the lecture George and I began to laugh and were unable to stop. It was almost as though, in the act of gazing
across the top of Emmeline's head, each had found a reflection of himself in the other's face.

Later, George somewhat ungallantly apologized for having been Emmeline's escort by saying, "Emmeline? She's
not my girl. She's a friend of one of my old girls." He
added, "It's the sweetheart of the corn I really like." Seeing
that his friends did not laugh at this joke, he clarified it. "I
mean the girl whose picture is on the cornflakes box: Belle
Minuit."

I heard the laughter, but it was not until a photograph
of a girl who, George thought, was my double had appeared
on the cover page of the *Police Gazette* that my resemblance to the shy country girl pictured on the cereal boxes
was clear to me. Immediately thereafter, George and I
began going steady.

At the end of our freshman year, Emmeline transferred
from Red Rock to Smith, and without her plump presence
the delightful absurdity of our first double date was lost.
This is not to say that George and I stopped laughing when
Emmeline left us. But our laughter changed from some-

thing shared to something that could not be shared, because we no longer understood it. Perhaps, like Pandora, I was created to punish another man. In any event, like Epimetheus and Pandora, we were married, and our troubles began on the morning of our wedding day when having gone into a jewelry store to buy a ring, it seemed for one awful instant as if George might desert me. I had made the mistake of choosing the more expensive of the two rings that were available in my size. As George opened his wallet a second time and added two dollars from it to the ten-dollar bill already in the jeweler's outstretched hand, he looked wilted, like a person who has lost an argument. In reality, there had been no argument; George, having begun his courtship with laughter, had pressed his suit with cheerful determination for six whole years. It was unthinkable that he had not wanted to marry me, after all. But how else could I explain his indifference to wedding rings? My father had not found it necessary to buy a ring for my mother, his splendid presence being sufficient evidence of his affection. Since then, however, rings had gained in symbolic importance, and George's reluctance to buy one caused me to feel for the first time in his presence — in addition to fear and admiration — anger.

But the tantrum George suffered on the morning after our wedding originated in a simple misunderstanding with the desk clerk about the cost of our hotel room and had nothing to do with me.

"I've been hooked," he said.

"Hooked?" I was surprised, naturally.

"Eight dollars is too much to pay for a room like this."

"On our wedding night?"

"What does that clerk think I am? A rube?" George, quite plainly, did not yet see himself as a married man.

I did not try to answer. "Don't shout, George. I think it's a nice room."

"You don't know the hotel business like I do. This is a rattrap." After which George looked at the bare walls of the room with the wide-eyed stare that a rat, if caught in a trap, might have had.

"See how neatly I've packed our suitcases," I said. "Let's go."

"I can't pay the hotel bill."

"Why not?"

"I don't have eight dollars."

"You don't?" I was too surprised to be either frightened or angry. My father, having said to those neighbors who sometimes teased him about being the father of an only child that "children are luxuries," had quite seriously proceeded to shape his paternal policies around this belief. And, having limited himself to a single luxury, he had been, as he often said with a smile, "an indulgent father." I grew up without realizing either that some of my acquaintances had more spending money than I did or that many of them, including George, had less. Since George and I were alike in so many ways, I had imagined that he too had had an indulgent father.

In fact, the financial difficulties of George's growing up, made more acute by the long illness that preceded his father's death several years before, were still so painfully clear in George's mind that real tears came to his eyes whenever, recalling that unhappy time he said, "Poor devil, why couldn't I have helped him? He didn't know how to earn a living and there we all were — waiting to be fed."

In our hotel room now, George's facial expression seemed to imply that I, too, had been there in his father's house — waiting to be fed.

Fortunately, my father had given us a check. So when George said that the money he had saved for our wedding trip was already spent, I was cheerful. "We'll cash my check," I said. "Why didn't you tell me last evening?"

"I didn't want to embarrass you," George said.

We cashed my father's check and paid our hotel bill, and boarded the morning train for Buffalo. Since George had recently visited Niagara Falls with a party of men and my father's check was somewhat less generous than we had expected it to be, we decided to spend the next night in Youngstown, Ohio, traveling from there in the morning to the village where we were going to live. The day was hot and bright, and I was wearing a brown woolen dress with narrow bands of fur on its cuffs and collar. With it, I wore a brown velvet hat that both Hedda Hopper and the Duchess of Devonshire might have envied. George was dressed in his new — especially heavy — navy gabardine. While we were waiting in the Buffalo station for the Youngstown train, an aging woman in a flowered summer dress who had been watching us for some time said, "You look lovely. But aren't you warm in those clothes?"

"We are, I guess."

"Aren't you sure?"

"Yes, I am — sure." Grateful for George's calm good

humor, I scarcely had noticed the rising temperature. Later in the day, however, while undressing in our hotel room, George and I had our first quarrel.

Our anger flared without warning, like the spontaneous combustion of a new crop of hay. Walking from the railway station with a suitcase in each hand, George had attracted the attention of some young men who, it seemed, had loitered in the dark shadow of the station for the purpose of directing us to a hotel. Noisily jocular, they surrounded us, making a joyful procession to the nearest street corner, where, together, we climbed into a crowded trolley car. There, peevish and perspiring, I said, "You should've called a taxi."

"A taxi? I like trolleys. Don't you?"

"No. They remind me of the horrors I've already survived."

"Horrors? What do you know of horrors?"

"Enough."

"You've never even been hungry. You've always had everything handed to you."

"Not *always*. And I have been hungry. I'm hungry right now."

At this point, seeing that we had arrived in the business section of the city, George said, "There's a hotel. Let's get off here."

I do not remember the name of the hotel in which we spent the night, nor can I recall the name of the place where we stayed the night before; all I remember is that in these hotel rooms I learned that even when two persons look as much alike as George and I do the difference in their way of seeing things may be immeasurable. To me the hotel was horrible. I said so, adding, "It is *my* money, after all, that we're spending."

"Didn't you mean to say 'my father's money'?"

"No. He gave it to me."

"Then it's mine, too."

"Yes, certainly, because I gave it to you. But I hate this hotel and riding on trolley cars at night."

"The room's clean, the bed looks strong. Those are the main things to look for in a hotel — cleanliness and a strong bed. Nothing is worse than a bed that lets you down with a bang in the night."

"Have you had much experience with such beds?"

At this, to my complete surprise, George's anger became quite frightening and his tone of voice so stentorian that if we had been on my grandfather's hilltop farm, the sound easily might have carried two miles. "*Who*," he said, "do you think you are? You're not the first girl I could've married. And, for all I care, you can go to hell. *This* is *humiliating*."

"*This is humiliating*." Not only had George had the last word; he had taken it right out of my mind and left me with nothing to say. I laughed then and got into bed. It was, it seems, George's great gift for guessing what I wanted to say and saying it that had brought us together — to bed in Youngstown, Ohio.

And I remembered that before our marriage when, after a long kiss, he said, "I'm an ugly devil," I had smiled because, from the acuity of George's insight, it was plain that his intentions were so far from serious that what our classmates took to be lovemaking was, in reality, nothing more than an attempt by one ugly devil to console another. Surely we did not expect to be married.

In the first month of our marriage, George tried to explain the circumstances that had changed our coincidental enrollment in Red Rock College into the complex reality of wedlock. It was after one of our quarrels. He said, "I married you because of your amusement value."

With memories of the unamusing behavior of those sober-looking women in dark dresses who had cared for me in my childhood and the sly laughter of the men who lived with them still clearly in mind, I supposed that the ability to laugh and provoke laughter was, along with woman, God's chief gift to man. The thought, therefore, that my "amusement value," if not really the only value I had, was the only one George valued depressed me — no matter how gently I turned it over in my mind. "But you said you wanted me to *help* you."

"I do want you to help me." Yet, at the same time he was speaking, George's mind was obviously busy elsewhere. And an instant afterward he said, "Boy, you should be in burlesque. If I could play trombone, you'd be there."

"I can't sing."

"You wouldn't have to. You wouldn't have to do anything."

"But I want to do something. I want to be a painter. I want to help you, too, and buy back my grandfather's farm. I want to do a little of everything." After which I said to myself, "And I don't want to be more amusing than wives commonly are, George."

"Then help me find another job."

"You have a job." He was superintendent of a small oil-drilling operation.

"Belle, we aren't living on my salary. We've spent your father's check *and* the money my brother gave us."

In September, George's suggestion that we should have been a burlesque team had seemed an amusing absurdity and nothing more. By the holiday season, however, whenever George sang, "Gee, I wish I were a single girl again," I wondered quite seriously whether he had picked the words from my mind. But if, a few minutes later, he said, "When poverty comes in through the door, love goes out of the window," my answer invariably was "That's nonsense, George. Don't say it."

Yet, like everything George said, it sounded like the truth. And the connection between George's repetition of this old saw and my failure to apply for a job as teacher in the local schools was clear in his next words: "You know what I'm earning."

"Yes. And we'll live on it."

"When?"

"When we've learned to live together. Money is secondary."

"You've never been hungry."

"I've always been hungry. I'm hungry this minute."

"You eat too much."

"I've never had enough to eat."

"You should've lived with us. We had wonderful meals at our house."

Conscience-stricken then, I thought of the burned chops

and the unsuccessful pilaf we had had for supper. "If you want a divorce, George, I won't contest it — or ask for alimony."

"The Adamses don't get divorces."

"There's never been a divorce in my family, either."

"Why not?"

"I don't know. My mother said that she often thought of getting one when she found out that living with my father wasn't pleasant."

"Why wasn't it pleasant?"

"She said he was a baby. And I don't think my mother is really fond of babies."

"Who is, Belle? Let's face the facts. Who can afford them?"

"Don't shout at me, George."

"Finish your story. I like both of your parents. But I think it was a shame they ever got married. Why did they stay together?"

"Mother's explanation was that I prevented her from going ahead with a divorce. Yet they had been married seven years before I was born. But of course that wasn't the only lie my mother told me. It never seemed to me that my father was a baby, either."

"Why did she marry him?"

"She thought he was a smart man, she said."

"That must've been the reason my mother married my father. But she was twice as smart as he was. She should've tried to earn a living for him. The poor devil. She should've tried to help him."

"Well, my mother helped my father. She peddled eggs

and potatoes from house to house in town when I was a little girl. And everything she earned she gave to my father. And when he thought he had enough money, he sold my grandfather's farm, which she loved, and moved my mother and me to town."

"It wasn't his fault," George said. "He didn't like the country, and he's happy now."

"I wish I could believe that. But I can't. And one day we are all going back to my grandfather's farm — you and I and my parents and the son we're going to have."

"Now I know why my mother didn't want me to marry you."

"Why?"

"Because, she said, you are an idealist and I'm a practical person."

"But that's why we got married, George. Isn't it?"

"No. *Hell, no.* And you know as well as I do that it wasn't. There's no *reason* in love. People get married because they don't know what else to do. People are much dumber than you can imagine, Belle. You just can't imagine how dumb people are. That's your only trouble, Belle. You wouldn't be any worse than the rest of us if you could imagine how dumb the rest of us are."

"Am I worse than other people, do you think?"

"Your thinking sometimes is out of this world, and the things you say don't always *sound* right."

"And that's the reason your mother fainted when the announcement of our wedding reached her?"

"No."

"No, she fainted because you, after debating the awful

prospect for six years, hadn't the kindness to tell her we were going to be married. How could you have done such a thing? You, George Adams, the *practical* one?"

I suspect that Emmeline, who had left Red Rock at the end of our freshman year in the hope of getting a degree from Smith, had guessed how things were going to be with us when, having failed to graduate that year, she came to our graduation exercises and told me, "The Adamses are *dreadfully* bankrupt, you know. Or did you know?"

"Yes, I know."

"Then you won't marry George?"

"Not for a long while. I'm going to graduate school next year. Anyway, George hasn't asked me."

Whereupon Emmeline, with a grin as wide as her face, said, "You certainly can do better. Don't marry George."

Poor Emmeline, I thought, how little you know me — forgetting that, before I knew him, she had known George. "I can't promise you that I won't marry him. But I'll always remember that you warned me."

After this meeting with Emmeline, my lively correspondence with her became less lively.

It was eight years later and I was pregnant when we met again. George and I were coming home from a visit to George's sister ("Now, if I should marry you, you must get along with my sister," George had said to me on a walk we had taken once when we were seniors; it was as close as we had ever come to discussing the possibility that we might marry), and we stopped off in Patterson to see Emmeline. It was a dark December day, with melting snow in the air and several inches of slush on the pavement, and although a number of persons had given us directions along the way, we had difficulty finding the office where she worked.

When we found her finally, Emmeline greeted us as though seconds instead of years had elapsed since she advised me not to marry George. Without saying "I told you so," she managed to suggest that my condition was plainly unfortunate. "What in the world have they done to you, child?"

Guessing that the pronoun referred to George and his family, I said, "Have I changed that much in eight years?"

"My dear, you don't look anything like you did."

Emmeline was not the sort of person with whom anything was to be gained by argument, since she was nothing if not truthful. So I simply said, "I know I shouldn't have worn this hat. Forgive me. It's more comfortable than it looks." I was wearing an old black hat George's sister had given me. It sat on my head like a black pot. I wore it for years.

Smiling then at George, Emmeline said, "*You* haven't changed."

"No, I'm the man."

George held his homburg close to his chest and his tall body taut — as though, the next instant, he might bow from the hips. His manliness, I thought, was self-evident. More than that, since Emmeline had noticed that my appearance had changed for the worse, it seemed to me that she should have seen how much George's looks had improved.

"George means," I said, "that we're going to have a baby."

"When, child?"

"About the first of April."

"Will you let me come to see him?"

"You must."

"It will be a boy?"

"Yes. We expect to have a boy."

Emmeline grinned at George and said, "I didn't know that Belle was prescient — in addition to all of the other things she is. Did you?"

"No. I can't imagine *why* she married me."

George's wit was often remarkably sharp. For, although it was because of certain foresights that I had married him, he did not know what they were until long after all of them had come true.

Eric was three months old when I saw Emmeline for the last time. She came without a word of warning and met me in the doorway of my parents' home — where we had moved to wait for our son — just as I was about to leave, after Eric's afternoon feeding, on an errand. Breathlessly I explained the urgency of my errand and its connection with the fact that on the next day George's mother was coming to spend some time with us — her second visit in the nearly seven years we had been married.

Dimpling, Emmeline said, "I've come to see your son. We're on the farm for the summer and Ethelbert brought me over."

I noticed then that a large car, with a man and an uncounted number of children, was parked in the shade of a horse chestnut tree.

"Have you driven a long way to get here?"

"Oh, no. Our farm is close to Mendelton. That's only fifteen miles from here."

"Then, since you're living in the neighborhood, I wish you would come again — when George and his mother are here. How about the day after tomorrow? I *have* to do an errand. Please come back another time."

"Ethelbert may not be able to bring me another time."

"Why don't you ask him?"

"I'd hate to do that. Summer vacations are so short."

Regretfully, I went back into the house with Emmeline, to the bedroom where Eric was sleeping, and stood beside her while she turned the experienced eye of a maiden aunt on him. More, she touched him with the firm hand of a maiden aunt and broke the sleep that otherwise might have lasted through the afternoon. Red-faced and dry of tongue, I lifted Eric from his crib and, after an unsuccessful attempt to stop his crying, returned him — damp and angry — to the crib. "Forgive me, Eric," I said. "Your grandmother will help you survive the afternoon. Don't cry too hard."

"Well, I certainly hope he will get some love from someone," Emmeline said.

Later in the afternoon, when I might have told her — but didn't — how it had happened that, contrary to her advice, I married George, she confessed to me that she currently was in love with a married man. Plainly glad herself, she seemed to expect me to be unhappy about it. And if, having already ruined my afternoon, she had said, "It's George, you know. I've always been a little in love with him," it would not have surprised me. More than that, I probably

would have laughed and told her that ever since the beginning of our freshman year at Red Rock I had suspected as
much. But Emmeline kept the man's name to herself and
let her ill-timed visit drag to its conclusion without laughter.
I regret our sober parting, because, oddly enough, we never
met again.

On second thought, perhaps it was better that the whole
truth — like the face of the Lord on Mount Sinai — was
"covered." Perhaps, like the people who had come with
Moses to the plain at the bottom of the mountain of truth,
we had said in our hearts, "Let not God speak with us, lest
we die." In any event, as the mother of George's son, I had
no real interest in Emmeline's predicament, and she, with
insight so myopic that she had seen Eric as an unloved
child, surely would not have believed the things I might
have, with laughter, told her. To ease the pain of our
many misunderstandings, my father had a habit of saying,
"The truth is so strange that I don't expect you to believe
it." The truth about the revelation that had left me with
no choice but to marry George and become Eric's mother
was, in fact, even more strange than truth commonly is. So
that poor Emmeline, hearing it, might well have doubted.

This is not to say that it is easy for me to understand, myself, the curious incident without which, almost certainly,
I would not have become the mother of Eric Adams. It
was a small thing, the sort of thing that Joan of Arc — or
almost anyone — might have heard when alone in a quiet
room. But I was not alone — not really. And I was out-
doors.

I remember the kind of day it was — the way the leaves

of the Carolina poplars smelled when I shuffled among them without lifting my feet, and the weight of books in my crossed arms. I remember the noisy boys in long raccoon coats and little cocked hats who were going in topless cars to the football game in Hamilton. And, seeing how carefree they were, it had been natural, I imagine, for me to see myself — standing alone on the windswept sidewalk, after a tedious morning in Clarke Library — with a melancholy clarity. My appearance, thanks to a generous allowance from my parents, was more posh than poor. And yet suddenly — above the singing and the roar of shifting gears — I could hear the words that my mother had repeated to me when I was a child: *"You will never be right."*

But now, instead of laughing and waiting, as I had as a child, for the familiar voice to say that I must not believe it, I seemed to be nodding in sober agreement. While the leaves spun in capfuls of wind from the trees that had shed them, I saw myself through the eyes of the unmentionable woman who had said the terrible truth when I was born. And I said to myself, "Yes, I know. No matter what I do, the ankle-length raccoon coat, the topless car, and the right to sing in them will never be mine. It is very sad."

Then, oddly, another voice said, "You aren't going to the football game today because you aren't *right*. But your son will go. Everywhere. Your son will be truly representative of the clan. Go back to your dreary little room with your books and forget the football game. You can't go with the boys. Never."

"But what must I do to have this son?"

"Marry George."

"Really?"

"Yes, why not? Do you know anyone else as well?"

"No."

"Can you think of anyone who wants to marry you?"

"No."

"Then be glad you know George. And marry him before he changes his mind about you."

So, contrary to Emmeline's advice, I had married George, because a son had been promised to me — as the honor price, *wergild, eric* — for my life. It was not the sort of bargain that Emmeline would have been able to understand, and perhaps it was just as well that a chance to describe my "revelation" to her never came. Poor Emmeline. What did she know of love?

The fact is that, even if she had asked me to express the joy and gratitude I felt, I would have had no words, and to have read the song of thanksgiving that begins with "For this child I prayed and the Lord hath given me my petition which I asked of Him," while true in itself, implied more than I meant to say; Hannah's willingness to lend Samuel to the Lord was a form of gratitude that I did not understand. My joy, however, was real. Eric's weight at birth was a spare six pounds and nine ounces. His hair, while dark, was neither black nor heavy. And instead of looking at me with the quickly averted glance that both George and my father habitually gave me, Eric looked at me steadily and calmly, as if I was *right*. Eric was a baby.

Suddenly, after many years of believing that I was wrong and, therefore, in constant need of correction, I was free to speak my mind without any dreadful precognition of my family's embarrassment. It was almost as if I, that rude daughter of the fairy tale from whose lips fell an assortment of toads and frogs, had become, when Eric was born, her blessed sister, whose words were diamonds and pearls. Confident that my every word would be welcome, if not infinitely precious, I lay in my hospital bed with a happily expectant air. Sometimes I laughed until my doctor, called by the alarmed nurses who were in attendance, ordered ergot and phenobarbital.

When I was well enough to have visitors, one of them said, "It was the anesthetic that made you laugh."

"No," I said. "I am happy. And it seems very *funny.*"

But she had never been married, and I don't think she believed me.

v

LOCKED INTO A STAR

ERIC'S BIRTH and my own were similar in one respect; each became the fifth member of a middle-aged quartet aged, on an average, forty-six years at the time of Eric's arrival and fifty-three when I was born. And by adding one to the divisor in both instances, we added almost ten years to the life expectancy of our parents and the grandparents with whom we came to live. Any infant, in the same circumstances, would have done the same thing. Yet I take comfort in this fact and suppose that Eric does too. Ten

years is a long time, whether you call it "a time of tribulation" afterwards (as my father often referred to the first
ten years of my life) or say (as Eric did in *The Dogwood
Tree*), "The five of us already there locked into a star that
would have shattered like crystal at the admission of a
sixth." Luckily for his parents and grandparents, Eric's
star was, in its small way, a navigational star.

No one, at the time, defined our condition in the words
that Eric, at thirty, used. And I doubt that we ever thought
of the circumstances that had brought the five of us together
as a "star." "Star: a heavenly body visible, or a point of
light" — as Webster's dictionary defines it — certainly
sounds pretentious. Yet there was an undeniable dynamism
in the light by which we saw ourselves, and each other,
quite plainly. What was more necessary to our survival, the
forces at work in us gave off considerable heat. So that we
were, in every sense of the phrase, "warmly human." Otherwise, I suppose, Eric might have used a less lively word to
describe the first thirteen years of his life. ("Moon," since
we know our satellite more intimately, is unthinkable.)

Eric excepted, each of us had a comparatively carefree
decade to remember — a time when my parents had lived
alone in their sunny suburban home and George had been
spared, by his job in the plant department of the American
Telephone and Telegraph Company, the worries associated
with what he refers to as "living in one place." In the six
years of our marriage, we had lived in many places from
which, depressed by the squalor of our temporary quarters,
I had retreated to my parents' house either at George's
suggestion or my own. Now George, jobless, had retreated

with me and Eric to my parents' many-windowed house, with its old-fashioned garden of fruit trees and grape arbors, and my mother had welcomed us by saying, "This house is big enough for five people." Later she often said, "Do you know that we're all babies? Isn't it nice that we get along so well?"

Since my parents and George were the youngest living survivors of their respective families, I supposed that their ability to tolerate two "only children" was a delight for which my mother's former complicity with nine older siblings had not prepared her. And when, occasionally, I felt a premonition comparable to the sensation a bird might have in its bones before a storm, I did not speak of it; it was pleasant to hear how much she enjoyed those personal relations that seemed to be, besides the house, our only asset. Happily we could not foresee that the amiability in which we then lived would ever change.

George had enrolled in Steuben College to ease the monotony of being in one place too long and Eric — no longer "a baby" — became "the young man." In an attempt to keep something of the happiness we shared that first year (in my father's many-windowed house), I made a few notes at the year's end (on the first day of Eric's second year) and said that his grandfather invariably referred to him as "the young man." It set the style for a friendship that lasted to the end of my father's life and, on that account, has a place in the record.

This record, dated March 19, 1933, includes a snapshot of "the young man" taken with George's mother on the day of his baptism. They are sitting together in a grass chair that was made in Hong Kong. There is a tall deutzia in their background and she smiles broadly while Eric points to the place where — on August 26, 1932 — his first tooth appeared. He understandably is anxious about the tooth and does not smile. Yet a family resemblance to his Grandmother Adams is clear. Seven months later, one of the baker's dozen of snapshots that still adheres to this small history book shows Eric and his Grandmother Minuit walking along the street in the direction of our house.

In this picture, too, Eric resembles a grandmother who is smiling broadly. The trellis I made for the clematis is their background and on its frozen vine there are tufts of snow. Eric is wearing his first pair of shoes (white) and a legging suit (red) that I knitted. The child — prophetically — leads my mother, holding the arthritic fingers of her right hand in his left and both bodies lean forward. Looking at the picture now, I see that this was not a leisurely walk — but *flight*.

The written record, after mentioning the fact that Eric picked a red cosmos from the border near the barn on August 28, 1932, skips September. It was a month for taking pictures, the only time when Eric was both blond and fat. And the written record is resumed on October the third, when Eric's grandfather administered the traditional aptitude test: a dollar, a cake, and a book. If the baby picks up the dollar first, the parents may expect him to become a wealthy man or, at least, the kind of man who is willing to be wealthy. If the book is his first choice, their son will be a scholar or a bookworm. In the event that the cake is chosen before either the dollar or the book, the parents can

prepare to feed the boy and hope for the best. Born a
woman, I presumably did not have this multiple choice
and watched Eric's decision with great excitement. We
sat around the dining room table while my father set the
test before Eric, and he, with one deft pincers' movement,
embraced the three objects simultaneously. Why my
record reads "Eric's first choice was the dollar, second was
the cake while with his left arm he embraced the book,"
I do not know.

It is not a wonder, however that Eric's first word was
"baby" or that I had nothing more to confide to "Mother's
Notes" until March 19, 1933, when the dogwood tree had
been planted. At that time, my tone is oddly breezy — a
tone I still use to prevent a flow of tears — and brimming
with *camaraderie*. It is as though, having given "the young
man" a firm pat on the back, I am suddenly his older
brother telling him how his first year was.

"And so goodbye to your baby days! You have fallen off
all the beds and rolled down some of the stairs. You have
brought twelve teeth into the world without whining. You
have taken your meals like a man and never complained
of anything but the dairy's milk. And now you are a busy
boy sitting on the floor playing with the typewriter — that
shouldn't be where it is. Perhaps you are learning something very useful. Who knows?

"Your father lost his job this first year of your life and
we have been worried for your sake and our own. But you
have laughed and grown and so, I hope, have your parents.
Yesterday we planted a pink dogwood to grow along with
you. The nurseryman said the tree might be ten years old

and made us pay five and a quarter dollars for it. But it will be priceless some day. I hope you will like it."

The planting ceremony had been attended by the five members of our household and quietly observed by the neighbors. Standing in the yard while my father dug a hole for the roots of the dogwood tree, I could feel that the weather was going to change. Indeed, we scarcely had planted the tree before it began to rain. And according to the daily weather report in my father's diary, the rain lasted three days.

My father reminded me that there are many more valuable trees than the dogwood. "And it is a short-lived tree," he added. "I would have planted something else."

"But I've always wanted a dogwood tree," I said. "Don't you remember?"

"Yes. I remember. And it died."

"You told me that it would die because the chain I used to pull it up had barked it all along one side of its trunk. It died slowly," I said, remembering the young tree's decline and death. "So the chances are that this tree will live a long time."

My father had lifted his newspaper then to show that our dialogue was over. My mother had returned to her rocking chair and was asleep. It was a long time since she had said, "George makes a person feel good with the things he says," and George, in jovial mood, had told a caller, "I married Belle because I like her mother. If she ever learns to treat me like her mother does, I'll be a happy man."

Differ though they did — in their ways of eating, sleeping, talking, working, and accepting the difficulties that surrounded us in the early thirties — both of my parents were genuinely fond of George. As they sat in the living room together now, my father was talking and — the newspaper folded beside his chair — listening with that special deference he ordinarily reserved for his own opinions while George spoke of Roosevelt's recent inauguration. Had my mother been awake and busy before the old-fashioned, black-topped sink, she might have said, "George knows how to make a person feel good. I never saw anybody like him."

So seldom, indeed, did the things I said to my parents seem to make them feel good that I envied George and, when the remarks he made in my presence were not pleasant, wondered why — having the gift to please — he had not shared it with me. When I asked him about the lack of gladness in some of his observations to me and he was either evasive or entirely silent, I assumed that our marriage, having passed its "familiarity breeds contempt" phase, was moving toward the turbulence that George had foreseen when he said, "I'm going to make your life *hell*, Belle, if I have to teach school."

Both possibilities had seemed so remote — with George enrolled in Steuben College and teaching jobs as scarce as other kinds of employment — that I had laughed and said, "You would never do that, George."

Having planted onion sets in my parents' garden on Roosevelt's Inauguration Day and, two weeks later, bought a pink dogwood tree to "grow along with Eric," I was prepared for anything George might do. And there is no hint, certainly, in the diary my father kept at this time, that George was less agreeable then. "About home all day," an entry that occurs frequently in all of my father's diaries, is followed, in the year we planted the pink dogwood, by "cloudy and threatening." But the only references to George relate to his attempts — Florida in September to see his mother and New York in December to visit his sister — to break the monotony of being in one place. On December 13, 1933, my father's diary reported: "Cloudy and cold. George went to work on grading." The "grading" was sponsored by the Work Projects Administration on the school ground adjacent to our house and there, early in January, my father joined George.

Watching the swirling clouds of ocher dust from a kitchen window, my mother and I congratulated each other on having helped to elect Franklin Delano Roosevelt, the man who had sent the Work Projects Administration to save us from going into debt to creditors other than each other. I had never seen either my father or George in one of their moments of elemental heroism — although I did not doubt, having listened to some of their conversation, that both had known such moments — and was as proud as the wife of any one of the soldiers at Valley Forge, in the winter of 1777, ever was. So that now, when I see (in my father's diary) that he failed to mention the fact that I was employed six months earlier in the drapery department. of Hartman's store, I smile, knowing that my job was not a source of pride to him.

What is more regrettable, Eric at first had cried whenever I left the house to go to work at Hartman's. My father's habit then had been to hurry away for his morning walk while, it seemed to me, he could have prevented "a time of tribulation" by inviting Eric to walk with him. Yet when I asked him to do this, pointing out the benefits to himself, myself, and my mother (for whom baby-sitting was a source of worry at best), he, smiling, said nothing. Both of these responses seemed unfortunate to me then and, even now, are a disappointment. Can it be true that my father — remembering Eden as a place where neither children nor their mothers needed to have their feelings soothed — really felt no obligation to be helpful? Or, having grieved for a little boy who was accidentally drowned while his mother was absent, was it too much to have expected him to associate that grief with Eric's tears and my anxiety? I still ask myself these questions. And, in the silence, wonder why my father smiled.

Eric was three years old when Emory Adams, who was going on four, died. Planting peas in the garden a few days later, I had an attack of angina that, in combination with the fact that both of the little boys we had expected to grow up with Eric were dead, caused me to resign my job at Hartman's store. The decision was made quite suddenly and used a syllogism based on the assumption that three is, in reality, a magical number toward which the number two inevitably turns. In other words, Eric had followed two little boys into this world and must — now that both of them were dead — die as they did. So convinced, I retreated once more to my father's house either, by my presence, to prevent Eric's death in early childhood or witness it. I scarcely dared to hope to see Eric a grown man, even when my hopes were highest.

And my hopes — when Eric was between four and five

years old — did sometimes rise to a point from which I
could *see* a second child in my father's house, a child that
would cheer and comfort us when Eric had gone to school
and, later, when I, at the age of sixty-five, slept in a rocking
chair (as my mother at this very moment did), would say
a comforting word to Eric. When I mentioned this pleasant
possibility to George, however, he said, "Another child?
Hell *no*. I've seen *enough* suffering. Haven't *you?*"

The voice was George's — without a doubt. But the pro-
hibition was my father's, based on a belief that children
(even though they, happily, have not added to the totality
of human pain by special defects of their own) may cause
suffering in innumerable ways.

And it seemed to me that I understood how my parents
had come, as my mother said, to be "afraid to have another
child." Under the circumstances — with everyone either
old, or ill, or in a state of shock on account of my oddity —
anyone might have been *afraid*. In Eric's case, however,
the assorted sufferings had been so far outweighed by joy
that when George said, "I've seen enough suffering," my
pride was as deeply hurt as Hannah's, I imagine, would have
been if Elkanah — seeing Samuel dressed in the little coat
she had made for him — had said the same thing.

"Where, George? Where?"

"Everywhere. Your blood isn't right. You should have
the kind of blood I have."

"That's nonsense. I don't want to be a superman."

"Then get a job — like other women."

"I have a job — like other women. I'm a mother."

"The kid doesn't have all of his buttons either."

"How do you know?"

"He doesn't act like other children."

"Is that so bad?"

"Yes, a person has to be like other people. That's what's the matter with you. Nobody understands you. They think you're a *snob*."

"I don't mind. I must be what I am. And so must you, George."

"I'm not a teacher, Belle."

"The principal thinks you're a diamond in the rough."

"I hate teaching. I'll make your life unbearable."

"I don't know what else you can do. Do you?"

"Are you going to tell Eric's teacher that psoriasis isn't a contagious disease?"

"Yes."

When Eric was in the first grade, psoriasis — after he had suffered the measles in March — took hold of his skin with such malevolence that I, who had developed my own hand-to-head relationship with that disease in puberty, began to understand what George meant when he said, "I've seen enough suffering."

In a less intimate way I knew, too, that to be "a diamond in the rough" was not what, if given a choice, George would have chosen to be. Yet I doubted that, after two years of unemployment, he would bolt from the schoolroom (as I had on a stormy afternoon when I was nineteen) or bring "hell" home to me (as he had threatened to do, in the event that he "had to teach"). The things he said to me in the privacy of our bedroom were less agreeable than I, from time to time, had anticipated. But when I complained of mental cruelty to my father, he said, "Let me tell you, Belle, I have known worse men than George."

"Really?" At thirty-four, it sometimes seemed to me that the only men I had ever known were George and my father — both chosen by my mother. But of course this was not entirely true. There had been several other men — all worse than George — and I had chosen him. Nor did I — now that George's time of mourning for his lost job should have come to an end and would not — really wish I had married one of the others.

My failure to become a teacher, however, came to mind when George, seeing that I was in bed and waiting for him to turn out the light, said, "Belle, you're nothing but a clinging vine." And I am glad that he said it with a look of surprise — as though the thought had been as new to him as it was to me.

But since there was no smile to suggest that he was thinking of a luxuriant growth of Japanese clematis or, perhaps, a grapevine, I clearly saw an oak in the poison ivy's fatal grasp and, once again, complained to my father. "George thinks I'm a clinging vine," I said.

"Some men would have left you, Belle. And I wouldn't wonder if George did — any day. Now."

I thought it was very odd that my father had felt George's disappointment to be connected, in any way, with our marriage; for, until lately, it did not seem to me that it was anything more than the sad loss of "the only job he ever really enjoyed." But now, regretfully, I had learned — and very surprised I was, too — of another source of sadness and it had to do with my failure either to have inherited or earned a fortune. This is not to say that my failure, in these respects, was unknown to us. George and I had discussed both sides of this failure almost daily in the first seventeen months of our marriage and — with the exception of Eric's first year — since our final retreat to my father's house. It is, however, a difficult subject and one that, even now, I must approach with a certain diffidence while George, looking back to a sadness we have somehow survived, says, "No, you weren't meant to be a teacher, Belle. You were meant to be Eric's mother. Nobody else could have been his mother."

Both the words and the way George repeats them comfort me — now. But I remember the first dress George bought for me and the way his eyes opened when he realized that my needs in clothing were an indication of my father's reliance on the Lord's love for "a cheerful giver" and nothing more.

The dress was, I thought, quite inexpensive and the color, henna, was George's favorite. Yet neither of us had enjoyed the dress because of its cost; both, in fact, had felt cheated and in the argument (was the price of the dress too high, or too low, really?) that followed my wearing of it George had said, "You're nothing but a false alarm, Belle."

"I am?"

"But I don't blame you. I blame your father."

"For wanting me to look *right*?"

"For not teaching you to face the facts."

"What were they, George?"

"That he couldn't afford to buy you the kind of clothes he did."

"Why should he have told me? I knew it."

"Then I blame you."

"For wanting to look *right*? For trying to look like a luxury — the only luxury he ever had or would have?"

A number of years passed before we again considered this curious failure in relation to "the facts." Then, right out of the depths of one of his unhappy reveries, George said, "Anybody who says that I married you for your father's money is a liar. I always knew he didn't have enough."

"Who said that you married me for my father's money? I want to meet them."

But George would not say more and I had the uneasy feeling that he, almost certainly, had been talking to himself.

It seemed most unlikely then — my failures notwithstanding — that George would ever say, "This house is too big for us." As Eric grew, there were times when, I thought, we needed more room. Previously owned and remodeled by childless couples, the house had become an impressive skeleton of hallways so that, in reality, we lived in a whispering gallery. And since my father and I were noise-haters and Eric, lacking a room of his own, slept in what might have been the master bedroom (if it had not become the way to the bathroom), the three of us needed *rooms*, if not more room. My father's share from Aunt Hester's estate had made it possible both to reduce the hall space (by building a new bathroom in the middle of the house) and turn the old bathroom into a bedroom for Eric. As it turned out, both of these innovations — like my former failures — had certain disadvantages. Scarcely had we noticed that Aunt Hester's gift had not been sufficient to equip the new room with a ventilator and, what was even more embarrassing, that my father had not parted with his inheritance as cheerfully as the circumstances had indicated, when George began to say, "Belle, this house is too big for us." And when I told him that it was, with the new rooms, just the right size for a family of five, he repeated what he formerly had said and concluded with "I'll leave you to stew in your own juice if you don't get out of this house."

Unable to imagine my life without George, I had begged him to stay and he had stayed. Yet I knew that the time for us to leave that house was drawing near. Eric was eleven. My first job in a war plant was finished and the tulips were blooming in the garden.

Feeling the familiar constriction of muscles that is at its best a heaviness in my chest and at its worst a struggle for breath, I reminded George of our unpaid obligation to my parents who had met us — whenever we retreated from other places — at the door of that house and shared their shelter and food and money. To which George replied, "They should've known better than to take in a pair of punks like us." And I had agreed.

The family doctor, too, agreed with George that it was time for us to move and, to facilitate our departure, sent a realtor to make my father an offer for his house. Sometime later, on a day when my breathing difficulties had put me to bed, the doctor made a house call. Backed by a high ramp of pillows and holding a drawing board in one hand and a pencil in the other, I said, "My parents are too old to move away from this house."

"And you're too old to stay in it."

"Old?" I was in my fortieth year but a long way from being old. At eighty, my father's strength had lessened a bit and a cataract had been taken from one eye, but neither the color nor texture of his skin were "old"; nor, I thought, had his way of walking aged. Mother, at seventy, was aging more noticeably. While George, as my mother had assured me twenty years earlier, was getting more handsome year by year. "I'm not old. Why should I be? Nobody else is."

"Yes," the doctor — who was ten years younger than my mother — said, "We're all old."

"Really?"

"Yes. You should live in a dry climate and a smaller house."

It was natural, therefore, that I should have begun to think of leaving my father's house. But the way it happened — like my first meeting with George — had an element of the supernatural in it. It is not strange, considering everything, that I spent the afternoon of the doctor's visit in bed, making sketches of small houses. The oddity was that, while thinking of building a small house in a dry climate, I had drawn a sketch of the house where I was born — quite unconsciously. Unlike the house in the suburbs — a tall construction of brick and wood in the Regency style, ostentatiously built by a man to impress other men — that house was designed by a woman to please other women. My drawing, poor though it was, recalled stone walls built to stand firm in stormy weather and a sunny succession of rooms that, miraculously, became a house without hallways.

"That is the only place I want to go," my mother said.

"If you move home again," Aunt Anna said, "We'll come and see you every week."

Death prevented Aunt Anna's weekly visits. But on the day of her funeral I, surrounded by a large party of mourners, made an announcement. "We're coming back to the old home place. Have the band out to meet us."

I had spoken so loudly that many of those who were present turned to gaze. And some of them, remembering the mistakes of my childhood, raised their eyebrows. Yet, less than a year afterwards, George and I bought the old Minuit place. It was as though a vine had uprooted the trees that supported it and transplanted them to another place. Out of the blue it had occurred to me that the farm was for sale. Who can say how it happened?

vi

A WOMAN'S HOUSE

ON THE FIRST DAY of the year (1909), my father wrote in his diary: "Clear and cold. Icy. Buried Mother." Then he added the undertaker's name and three words: "Nephews were bearers." Five days earlier, on the last Sunday of the previous year, his entry reads: "Clear not cold. Was home all day. Bart was here. Mother very poorly." So that a reader turns the page without being too much surprised by the words he wrote on Monday. "Clear and pleasant. Henry Glass was here. Augustus Glass repaired cellar door.

Mother died 8:08 A.M." Since my grandmother Mary died shortly after sunrise, I assume that the visit of Henry Glass and the repairing of the cellar door by Augustus Glass came somewhat later in the day than the diary suggests. We know for certain that the baker came that day, too, because the diary recorded this: "Rec'd of H. Glass $1.70. Bread $.28." It is as though my father — knowing how vulnerable his natural generosity and verbosity made him in a family that had little to say and only its physical needs to share — was determined to exorcise both in his diary.

Confined to her room (this room) because of physical failings that my father ascribed to a lack of memory and my mother to willfulness — although to me, now that I think of it, it seems to be more likely that my grandmother's failings had begun with a failure of her will — we never joined forces in the ways that the very old and the very young, living together, often do. So that I have no recollection of her presence during the four and one-half years we lived together and regret the fact that my father's diary deals so summarily with her death.

In my bedroom now there is a caned chair, commonly called a grandmother's rocker, that used to be hers. And when I am alone — wondering how it happened that we, in spite of being members of the same small household, were not acquainted — the chair seems to rock a bit. Looking through its caned back, I see the snowy slope beyond the road and the potted geranium on the windowsill. There is no one in the rocking chair. And I sit in it — only to find that I am too tall to be comfortable in my grandmother's rocker.

Going through the doorway from my room into the room that, after sixty years, still seems to be hers, I see the small coins of green paint, dropped by an unknown painter, on the wide bare boards of the floor and remember that when I visited this room, after her death, its wooden trim was painted a soft green. In memory it is the color of the meadow. And my repeated attempts, forty years later, to cover the green trim with white paint have broken the tie that once held this room to the meadow. Neither green nor white now, the room's wooden trim belongs less to the land and more to those houses where my youth was lost.

The headboard of the new bed, however, is low enough to give an unobstructed view of the meadow. Otherwise her room is, I imagine, much as it was on New Year's Day in 1909. Certainly, the doors of the jelly cupboard (to the left of the fireplace) stick, as they always did, to thwart the curiosity of visitors who would open them and the Adam mantel still gives a beauty to the little room that is both prim and unexpected. Those visitors who have tugged at the unyielding doors of the cupboard sometimes say, "This room does have an air about it."

Nodding and smiling, I say, "This is a woman's house. My father used to say that a woman *built* it. But since she was married and had a son, she must've had some help. All we know about her, really, is her name — Ann Gordon. It was her son Jacob Gordon — and I like to think he waited until she was dead — who sold the house, with eighty acres of land, to my grandmother's Uncle Dan on the first day of April, 1834."

Going to the window that used to be blocked by the

headboard of my grandparents' bed, we look down on the tree-ringed meadow. "It's lovely," the visitor says. "Don't let anyone take it from you."

And I assure her that death alone will take the meadow from me. It is a foolish promise, all things considered, but for the moment envy is inconceivable and death more acceptable than life elsewhere.

The meadow has the hypnotic beauty, if not the magic, of a crystal ball. Gazing into it from the window of my grandmother's room, I can see the child I was in the spring that followed her death. I am running to the house with flowers in both hands. I feel a need to run — lest the flowers wilt on the way. It is April and the broken sod is heavy with bluets.

The flowers vary with the time of year and my age: bluets in the spring when I was almost five, yellow fringed orchis in August when I was twelve, cardinal flowers in the summer of when I was fourteen. And always, under the matted meadow grass like autumn leaves, the orange-spotted turtles drifted and blinked their amber eyes at me. Now the bluets, orchis, and cardinal flowers are gone and golden ragwort, white campion, and tall meadow rue have taken their places. But the turtles are there, hiding among the stems of ironweed and swamp sunflower where the doe comes to feed her fawn at dusk. Watching them from my grandparents' bedroom, I try to count the deer that feed in the meadow without ever being sure of their number because the fawns soon become yearlings and the hunters take them away. The doe that had twin fawns in the woods last May is gone and I saw her go. Her fawns followed, the one walking lightly on the snow behind the other, and they have not come back. December is harvest time for the deer, as it was for my grandmother, Mary. Their hunters are noisy and jubilant as I was while the preparations for her funeral were made. Yet all that I know of her has been learned later — from my syzygy with this house and her furniture.

How much more — or less — I might have learned if I had not been born in Ann Gordon's house is hard to imagine. Nor, indeed, shall I waste what's left of my sense of wonder in guessing what my mother was thinking when (sometime after my grandmother's death) she said, "You were such a good baby, Belle — always laughing and singing in your cradle — and I didn't want her to spoil you. You never cried."

In memory I say nothing. I am both pleased and incredulous.

"But if she had *rocked* you, you would have *cried*."

And so, her willingness to be my baby-sitter dashed, my grandmother had retired to her room above the meadow and left me — laughing and singing — alone. *Alone* because the pride she took in my good humor, quite naturally, never compelled my mother to be its captive audience. Without an audience, therefore, we may assume that I soon stopped "laughing and singing" and became the solemn child who, in both size and modus operandi, seemed "odd" to a great many of her acquaintances. Plainly determined to offset this turn of events, my mother said, "You were such a good baby, Belle. What makes you so naughty now?" Later, since an acceptable answer to this question had not yet occurred to me, she said, "Stop that, Belle. If you don't, I'll whip you." And from time to time, she did.

The whippings, oddly enough, are not associated with those misdoings that I recall. An invasion of the cupboard, for example, where my grandfather kept his whiskey and cigars and the unsteadiness of my legs that sent my mother's hired girl into spasms of laughter had not required a whipping. Nor was I punished when, in the hope of being helpful, I reminded an aging visitor (who was sharing my grandfather's whiskey in the privacy of my grandparents' bedroom) that it was time for him to go home. Then, as though that verbal suggestion were not enough, I had taken his cane from its place beside his chair and removed it to a point near the gate that, ordinarily, marked the beginning of his homeward journey. None of this had seemed "odd" to me, but rather the outward expression of my goodwill toward all men but especially my father who, by this time, was ready to wish this guest Godspeed. It seemed so odd to this guest, however, that he never visited us again.

Since the outcome of that early error in judgment was an end of that old man's friendship with my family, it seems, in retrospect, to have ended the laughing-and-singing time of my life and marked the beginning of a time of learning to see those wonders of the woods and farm that, even then, turned the wonder of my many whippings into the trivial diversion my mother intended. Between the times when I was whipped and those times when, quite inexplicably — my naughtiness notwithstanding — I was not, I wandered in the woods and my grandmother's garden. Bouncing Bet and cabbage roses still grow where the whitewashed gate once was. Her snowball bush and pale lavender lilacs, too, have survived the sixty years since her death and are thriving. But it is increasingly difficult to see the ghost of a plump little woman sowing beans and beets in that plot of ground where chicory now blooms in such profusion.

"I turned this ground for Mother many times." It is the sound of my father's voice and his presence is both real and smiling. And I am glad to listen because my grandmother and I, although natural allies, were strangers in Ann Gordon's house. "Nothing, Pappy used to say, could've made Mother sell this place. But she would've stayed at the tavern a little longer, I think."

We — my father and I — are standing in the coarse grass, with chicory blooming at our feet. He is in his eighty-third year and I, on this day, am forty-two years old. It is the first summer of our return to this place and it seems natural to be thinking of my grandmother Mary. "Why do you think she wanted to stay at the tavern?"

"They were making a little money there. But Pappy had the night sweats and wanted to get out of the barroom. I don't think he would've left the farm if they could've made a living there." He is speaking of the farm where my grandfather was born — and his father died at the age of fifty.

"It is a beautiful place, I say."

"But hard to farm. He was thirteen when my grandfather died."

The prosperous-looking stone buildings and the fields that roll up and away from them on all sides come clearly to mind. "What a shame."

"Yes. My mother worked very hard there. When my baby brother died and they had to borrow the money to bury him, they left. Pappy often said that he thought a doctor might have saved the baby." He had not said, "There was no money to pay a doctor." "Then they decided to move to the tavern. And they made a little money there. Mother would've stayed a little longer, I think." Melancholy touches my father's face at this point and I guess that he, too — loving his fellowmen as the surfer loves the surf — had wanted to stay at the tavern a little longer.

Certainly, when we began to plan our return to the farm where I was born, my father had regarded the move as a retreat from life itself and said, "I'd rather die than go back to that place."

With equal spirit — since I thought that our survival depended on this move — I told one old friend who had a premonition that my parents were "too old" to be "moved": "We're moving back to the farm — if it kills us *all*." Then, realizing that my desperate vow included Eric, I had been frightened. Now that we had moved without a mishap and I could see that the oldest member of the family was in a good humor, I said, "It was a wise move, wasn't it?"

"Nothing, Pappy said, would've made my mother leave here."

"It's a woman's house."

When it first occurred to me that houses, although invariably feminine in France, can be both male and female in the United States, I was comparing my grandmother's house in the country with my father's house in the suburbs, a straight and narrow building that surely is more masculine than feminine, and recalling how uneasy my mother was when the widow who sold that house to my father said, "I hope you'll be happier here than I was." (She was, in fact, deserted by her husband somewhat as George — a lifetime later — threatened to desert me.) Then, opening the door of her son-in-law's bedroom and sniffing, she had told my mother, "I hate that smell. It's *him*." And, oddly enough, her son-in-law's scent remained to the end of the time my father and mother lived in the house.

Even more oddly, I think, my mother decided to make that room her bedroom and, in the twenty-three and one-half years of their occupancy, my father's voice could be heard at all hours of the night in what had seemed to be an angry monologue — since my mother seldom spoke — on the subject of men's rights. In fact the mildly pungent odor to which the widow had called my mother's attention, with propriety, might have been called *l'homme dans le piège*. Indeed, when George discovered his own considerable gifts (as a monologist) he sometimes concluded with cries of "I'm trapped. I'm trapped." And my mother and I, listening to both my father and George, wondered whether or not we were as happy as the widow who, having sold her house to my father, had wished us well. But of course the widow's wish for us had come true: we were happier than she had been because, having listened to our husbands, we were not entirely abandoned. And when my mother and I agreed to leave that house, having closed our ears to my father's cry of "It's a mistake. A mistake," they left with us.

The times when he, angrily protesting my decision to buy back the old Minuit place, had said, "Belle, it's a mistake. We're jumping from the frying pan into the fire," were already drifting away to the limbo where vexations of the spirit go. This, after all, was not the first time my father had moved — somewhat unwillingly — into the house Ann Gordon built. And now, standing where my grandmother's second garden had been, my father's speech lapsed into the style of his diary. "It was the third of April, 1873. The weather was clear and cold. There were snow banks along the lane. In the upper road I thought the wagon could not pass the chestnut trees. I was nine years old."

The chestnut trees had been a source of food when I was nine. And, having been born in their shade, my fears had to do with chestnut blight and other visitations from the outside world. "But you did pass the chestnut trees safely?"

"Yes. For many years, however, we had neighbors who asked me, 'Well, Jamey, how do you like living in the forest?' "

"What did you say to them?"

"I tried to be polite."

The politic silences of our sons were not the only parallels between my grandmother's acquisition of Ann Gordon's house and mine. In each instance there had been a party of five, with one of the number in exile from an urbanity that was very dear to him. She was forty-three years old and I was forty-one. My moving followed Hiroshima and hers, after close to a decade, the battle of Gettysburg. But, with the exception of Eric, we were (in the words of our family doctor) "all old," while she had been the only member of her family above forty years of age.

It is not her superficial resemblance to a poetess, however, that interests me now, but the stubborn smile that, thanks to a patient photographer, has lasted a hundred years.

"She was disappointed," my father said.

"How? Look at the lace gloves she is wearing."

"She was *proud*."

I look at the lace gloves that seem to magnify her heavy-boned hands and smile. They are my father's hands — and mine. The hands with which we have "worked very hard" without earning measurable wealth. "How was she disappointed? She never expected to be rich, did she?"

"There was someone she would've married — before — and she always thought somebody had lied to him."

At which point Victorian delicacy, it seems, required my grandmother to cover her hands with black lace and marry my grandfather. I wonder whether my father, ordinarily able and willing to supply all of the missing facts, is now prevented, by that same kind of delicacy, from doing so. Fortunately my grandfather, too, had his picture taken on their wedding day and all that I need to know is revealed by it.

Certainly, if he was the one who "lied" about my grandmother, his daguerreotype shows no sign of regret — only the determination that a tall, dark, and handsome man of twenty-five might be expected to feel on his wedding day. His straight hair is worn long (in a style that was revived a hundred years later by similarly handsome young men) and his bold glance meets the camera with a steady twinkle. And in this picture my grandmother's pride becomes real to me, so real that I think she could not, at the same time, have been "disappointed."

Holding her picture now, I can feel the obstinacy that my mother feared and, by keeping my grandmother's foot from the rockers of my cradle, would have discouraged in me. Looking at the plain oval face, I can hear that antebellum photographer urging her — as photographers since then have often urged me — to smile. And she does. But it is the Mona Lisa's smile without the Mona Lisa's beauty. The soft hair, parted like old-fashioned draperies, shows a high forehead and melancholy eyebrows.

Remembering my grandparents' daguerreotypes, I wish that George and I had not been too distracted on our wedding day to be photographed. My father's diary, interestingly enough, says: "Clear and pleasant. I went to the pheasant farm. George was here." George, as a matter of fact, had stayed until the next morning because it was our wedding day and we planned to take an early train. On that day the diary reads (and it is not easy to read because the words jostle each other): "Clear and warm. At noon I went to work and did not stay." This is the diary's tactful way of telling me that, on this date, my father decided to quit his job. Later it mentions a trip into the country, engine trouble, and the name of a neighbor who towed my parents back to the suburbs. The usual listing of expenses is appended. "Postage: $.09. Gasoline: $.38. Belle: $175." The latter was the check that George and I had found disappointing and cashed in haste before boarding a train for Buffalo on the following day.

Since, in retrospect, it seems that "disappointment" is to be expected at weddings, I still wonder why, with smiling satisfaction, my father said, "She was disappointed." The satisfaction — to me — was that my grandmother and I — at last — had joined forces in the house that "Ann Gordon built."

vii

TRANSLATION

My MOTHER knelt with my grandfather's right hand on her
hair while the rest of us, rubbing elbows in the quadrant that
had one post of the big, black bed for its focus, waited. Afterward, my mother was pleased to have been given "the blessing" and often spoke of it, while we, naturally, were somewhat disappointed that he hadn't also blessed us. At any
rate, I was. For in a summer day, a small tomboy can do
things besides reading in a darkened house to a dying man
with a penchant for Psalms — and I must have done almost

all of them — yet it was the daily reading of the Bible that I remembered when the summer was over, and I thought my grandfather would say that he remembered it, too. But, having blessed my mother and spoken, finally, to my father and his older sister, my Aunt Hester, he shut his unseeing eyes and did not, to my knowledge, open them again until the next day.

Then, to everybody's surprise, my grandfather sat up in bed and asked my father to bring him a glass of Old Overholt, and my father, even more surprisingly, brought him a glass of new cider instead.

But my grandfather, holding his head high, sniffed and again asked for a drink, so my father, who disliked delays and surprises about equally, had to fetch it from the tavern.

"He can't last that long," my father said, when he was back in the kitchen.

And my mother, noticing how red my father's face was all of a sudden, said, "Take your time."

It seemed to me that he did. But my grandfather waited without a word and having emptied his glass, died. After the impact of this, the funeral services were a sad letdown. The church was strangely warm and empty, as railroad stations sometimes are after a train has passed, and much of the food that the caterer had brought to our house to make a feast for my grandfather's friends had to be taken away.

"All of his friends are gone," a neighbor said. "Seventy-nine is a good age."

Now, we have no way of knowing, but it may have been his father's death that made my father first realize the possibilities of translation. We were much older, however, before hints of his determination to leave this world alive began to crop up in his conversation with us. He was in his early eighties and had been retired a few years from his day laborer's job with the road gang when — without preamble or provocation of any kind — words like these began to drop from his lips: "I didn't shed a tear for either one of my parents, and I don't want you to have a funeral for me."

One time he stopped, as though to study the effect of his confession and juxtaposed charge. And, inwardly shaken, I tried to think of something suitable to say.

The fact that he had not wept for his parents was not surprising to me. I had no tears for them. Nobody, as I remembered it, did. To my four-year-old way of thinking, my grandmother's demise, with the odors of carnations and freshly baked raisin pies blending and my father deferring to my grandfather's wishes in everything and the house alive with visitors, was delightful in every way (perhaps *delirious* comes nearer to the truth) and my pleasure was quite apparent.

My mother's high forehead had four or five horizontal lines that came and went with changes in her feelings. The lines were there when she put me to bed on the night before my grandmother's funeral. "Aunt Hester thinks you are a naughty girl," she said. "Are you? Did you get into the clothes basket while Aunt Hester was ironing?"

"Yes."

"Why?"

"I wanted to show her what the robin does."

"But you got in again after she had filled it with the clean clothes?"

"Yes."

"Why?"

"She knuckled me. Real hard. And I said I hoped she would be shot in the five-o'clock train. Real loud."

"That was naughty," my mother said.

The lines, however, were gone from her forehead and the day seemed to have ended well. Looking back, I find it puzzling that anyone but Aunt Hester could have misunderstood my wish to be entertaining at a sorrowful time, and yet the number that agreed with Aunt Hester was formidable — including, I suspect, my father, who was even now, thirty-six years later, trying to read my mind.

"But the laws require a funeral," I said.

"You know what I mean," he said.

"No."

"A man should leave this world in a whirlwind, like Elijah did."

"If we had a choice," I said, "I'd ask to be hung from a tree — after I'm dead of course — and eaten by the birds."

"And no memorial service?"

"My survivors can remember, or forget. I don't really care."

This was perverse of me, because I knew how highly my father prized the possibilities of memory. But he looked so well — so contemporaneous — that the thought of surviving him seemed preposterous. When he was eighty and I was forty, I had, after all, been mistaken for my own mother, and the mistake, I had persuaded myself, was due rather to the fact that my father looked only half his age than to the chance that I was looking twice mine.

Then, suddenly, my father was ninety years old, and my mother came to say that he wanted to see me. I went up to his room and stood in the doorway.

"Belle, I believe I'm dying," he said.

"But you can't." I laughed, remembering what he had said about leaving us in a whirlwind. "It's your birthday."

"Sit down, Belle. I want to talk to you."

My father was sitting on the edge of the bed, in a faded nightshirt. The illness, still new, had not affected his appearance enough to support the gravity of his announcement. Indeed, nothing did.

Seeing how lightly his feet touched the floor, my thoughts returned to the times when, somewhat unpredictably, a footbath took place. My mother and the rest of us washed our feet unceremoniously in the privacy of the bathroom. But the washing of my father's feet, being a family project with religious significance, could happen in any room of the house, and as a child I was usually present. It was, in a way, the only time when my presence seemed to be needed; some of the cozy connotations implicit in a robin's nest or clothes basket were expressed in my father's footbath. For when the temperature of the water in the basin, tested by the forefinger of one parent and the heel of the other, was pronounced "right," we three became, miraculously, *right* again — remaining in complete accord until both of the plump white feet had been dried and returned to my father's shoes.

Nearing the ritual's end, my father often quoted a part of the fifteenth verse of the tenth chapter of Paul's Letter to the Romans: "How beautiful are the feet of them that preach the gospel." Here, the more important half of the exclamation still to be said ("and bring glad tiding of good things"), he stopped short, with one flawless white foot in the air. It was an impressive sight — and one at which my mother and I smiled nervously. Compared to ours, my father's feet *were* beautiful.

Even now, resting side by side on the floor in the early sunshine of the day he was ninety years old, my father's feet had the look of complete innocence and, moved by the sight of them, my mother said, "Pop, will you let me wash your feet?" Then, hearing no protest, she went to get the basin.

While we waited, a pair of cicadas raised their voices in the walnut tree. "Nothing left now but the cicadas," he said. "Where are all the birds?"

"Nobody knows where the birds go in August," I said.

"I haven't heard a bird this summer."

"You couldn't have been listening." The truth is, I had not really heard birdsongs before the age of twelve, and now that I was forty-nine heard them much less clearly than I did at eighteen, when my need to hear them was so great that it was scarcely worthwhile for my parents and teachers to speak to me at all. This kind of hearing loss was to be expected by everybody who lived long enough — and my father had lived that long. At the same time, I was startled to hear him say it.

"When will the doctor come?"

"Around ten, I guess."

He sighed deeply and asked where my mother was.

"To get water to wash your feet."

"Pshaw." Careful to avoid the usual imprecations, he had learned to use this mild expletive with all but the direst results of true blasphemy. "My feet aren't dirty."

"Then the washing won't hurt."

"No, not you," he said.

My mother came then with the teakettle and a basin of steaming water. Setting the two vessels on the floor, she knelt beside them, and, after she had poured cold water from the teakettle into the basin, the testing got under way. Although my father said "Right," this time the miracle of communion did not follow, and the ceremony itself seemed to end more abruptly than usual. One of the flawless feet twitched, as if its owner had been tempted, fleetingly, to raise it for our edification. But no one dared to recall our little joke from Paul's Letter to the Romans, and my mother, admitting that my father's feet "were not really dirty," quickly dried them. Seeing that she did not return them then to the high-topped black shoes, I imagined that she must have known from the beginning how ill my father was.

Four hours later, the doctor told us. "There's nothing I can do," he said.

Accustomed to thinking of himself as a man of such benignity that he lived with women because it gave *them* pleasure and comfort, my father probably saw the prospect of a long illness in their care as the least pleasant of all the remaining possibilities. It was as though Elijah, having saved the widow and her son from slow death in Ahab's parched land, had been left to die in Zarephath — a man abandoned by God to the uncertain mercies of a woman.

It was unthinkable. And so, with an aplomb born of shock, my father answered everyone who inquired about his health in pretty much the same way: "I think I'm feeling better today" or "Things might be a lot worse. I have no pain." He remembered, of course, that Elijah had not been fatally stricken in Zarephath, or anywhere else, but had, because of his faith, been translated in a whirlwind to a happier place. My father never presumed to speak of Heaven, and yet obviously he wished to escape from the familiar place where he was.

Mistrusting women, he had no one to wait and watch with him as Elisha had waited with Elijah — since our Eric, his only grandson, was gone, so unfortunately, and married. My father had, almost certainly, counted on the boy to be on hand at the end, to take up his "mantle." The prophetic spirit he saw as already having been given to Eric in a double portion, according to the pattern set by Elijah and Elisha, and as now being dissipated in what my father jovially called "pleasing a wife." Eric's marriage, in short, upset his grandfather's plans in a way that was both shocking and lasting. And my father, alone with us, mentioned Eric less frequently. Every day, we had less to say to one another.

August had turned into September when, suddenly, our growing silence was broken. It was the day of Eric's homecoming, his first since the wedding; he was coming with his wife, and his wife's mother and father, to make us a visit. It was a warm and sunny day with the scent of fox grapes in the air. And my father, unable to hear the birds during the summer, could hear them plainly now.

"What kind of bird is that, Belle?" he said.

"I'm sorry. I didn't hear it."

He expressed no surprise. There had been too many failures on my part to hear and see and feel as he did. Sometimes, when exasperated by one of these shortcomings of mine, he said, *You are too sensitive.* And no irony, I believe, was implied — only a hint of man's original surmise about woman.

"Eric will be here this evening," I said. "He's coming to see you."

"With his wife?"

"Yes."

He closed his eyes then. And the way he sighed reminded me of my grandfather's death. The fact that soon, with Joan and her parents, we would be a party of eight suggested the bedside scene. The late-summer warmth, the insistent katydids, and the small bright room made a perfect setting for the death of a patriarch. With a minimum of imagination, I could see Eric on his knees, with my father's wide right hand on the tousled hair and the rest of us in a half circle at the foot of the bed. Afterward, Joan's father, a clergyman, might bless us all — for surely, by evening, we would all be in need of a kind word well spoken. But even while I imagined these things, I knew they wouldn't happen.

The spirit of a patriarch differs, no doubt, in many ways from the prophetic spirit, and my mother, unaware of these differences, was totally unprepared to do for my father what she had done so well on the day my grandfather blessed her.

"You may be enjoying yourself, Lucy," my father said to her. "But I want to go home." His voice was strong, suddenly, with the overtones of despair that had frightened me, from time to time, as a child. "Where is the other lady?" I was no longer Belle, the puzzling child, but another woman — not yet familiar enough to have a name, though both interest and affection were implicit in the question.

"She's busy." Mother's voice sounded gruff — certainly less girlish than it usually did.

This was not true. The house was shining and the food ready. But since Eric would be home in a matter of minutes, it seemed only sensible for me to wait downstairs until he came. Then, Joan and her parents welcomed, Eric could go to my parents' room and, seeing Eric, my father might immediately realize the utter impracticability of his wish.

"Belle!"

The sound of my father's voice was so close to the supernatural that I was afraid and, already hidden from him, could not answer. I wonder now why this was so. It seemed wrong for me to speak just then, and now it seems downright wicked that I did not. Yet, having decided to wait for Eric, I stood in the doorway and watched the road until I heard a heavy sound overhead.

Then I ran upstairs and opened the door of my parents' room — the room from which, until my father's illness, I was by tacit agreement barred. It is comforting to remember how they were — half smiling, with linked arms, and sitting on the floor at the foot of their bed.

"Of all things!" I said. "What are you two doing?"

"We are sitting on the floor." There was no way of knowing that these would be my father's last words. His tone was so truly matter-of-fact and conversational.

"Aren't you ashamed?" It was a foolish question and, like a great many of the questions I asked him, was never answered. Obviously, he had been trying to find me, and my mother had managed somehow to stop him. Death came while I chided him.

In a very short time, Eric arrived. With tears still undried, I said, "Grampy *died*."

"I know, Mother. I know. It happened as we turned off the turnpike. I felt him going."

"You did?"

"Yes. May I see him?"

When he came downstairs, Eric said, "He died *well*."

The words sounded so odd that I had to laugh. "It's the thing our family does best of all," I said. "We *do* die well, don't we?"

Perhaps I had expected Eric to be able to see the chariot of fire and feel the whirlwind and show me the mantle. At any rate, the funeral was as nearly "no funeral" as we dared to make it, and both Eric and I wept.

viii

THE MANTLE AND OTHER BLESSED GOODS

"MANY UNTOWARD THINGS can I remember, such as happen to all who live upon our earth . . . I can also bring to mind some pleasant goods and some inestimable evils, which, when I turn my thoughts backward, strike terror in me, and astonishment that I should have reached this age of fifty eight."

Since Benvenuto Cellini was born on November 3 in 1500, I assume that he wrote those words when he was fifty-eight years old and in a state of mind that is familiar to many — if not all — writers of autobiography. The "terror" and "astonishment" I have felt derive from memories as different from Cellini's, I imagine, as our natural heterogeneity and the lapse of four hundred years could have made them. And while the "inestimable evils" and "pleasant goods" he recalled and those "unexpected vehicles" mentioned in one of Eric's letters sixteen years ago, are not at all alike, all are oddly familiar.

It goes without saying that even when the inestimable evils and pleasant goods represent two sides of the same vehicle, the resulting wonder may lead to separate celebrations. For example, Eric only, seeing his grandfather dead on the floor, had thought of saying, "He died well."

A few minutes earlier, my own astonishment and terror had prompted me to say, "Please, God, be kind to him. We weren't." And now it was as if my guilt, previously unsuspected, had been written on the evening sky where Eric, seeing it, would have erased all thought of my shame.

Sometime later a former acquaintance, on hearing of my father's death, told George, "He always was a kind of creeping Moses."

We have no proof, however, that we are being truthful when we say, "Eric has taken his grandfather's mantle." In this time of neo-anarchism, that is a fanciful thought and very difficult to prove. Yet I remember a certain warmth — present in my father's lifetime — that now is gone. Repeating a droll expression he often used, we say, "There is an absence of heat." And because the existence of hairy mantles for Bedouins of all ages (from the prophet Elijah's time to our own) is a fact, we believe that my father had a "mantle," invisible and insubstantial as the religious beliefs of his family and friends, that Eric (like Elisha) received. In any event it is right that he should wear the garment that once warmed us all.

In the year after my father's death, my mother's health worsened and Eric, remembering her birth date, wrote as follows: "Sorry to hear that Grammy is down another notch. Yes, we are praying for you. I suppose any card of my own wouldn't make much of a dent, so this afternoon I'll buy and send the biggest and brightest card I can find.

"Joan has been sewing with the thimble marked L.Z.K. and it is as bright a thing as you could wish to see. The most lively-looking piece of silver I've ever touched. In what unexpected vehicles are we projected down the ages!"

Since then, Eric has written of his grandmother's thimble and my father's "translation" as if both — the astonishing life of the silver and the "terror" of my father's death — were cut from the same piece of "blessed goods." And who can say, with certainty, that they were not?

Interestingly, I think, Eric begins the story "My Grandmother's Thimble" with a confession and ends with prayer.

But we would-be novelists have a reach as shallow as our skins. We walk through volumes of the unexpressed and like snails leave behind a faint thread excreted out of ourselves. From the dew of the few flakes that melt on our faces we cannot reconstruct the snowstorm.

The other night I stumbled downstairs in the dark and kicked my wife's sewing basket from the halfway landing. Needles, spools, buttons, and patches scattered. In gathering the things up, I came upon my grandmother's thimble. For a second I did not know what it was; a stemless chalice of silver weighing a fraction of an ounce had come into my fingers. Then I knew, and the valves of time parted, and after an interval of years my grandmother was upon me again, and it seemed incumbent upon me, necessary and holy, to tell how once there had been a woman who now was no more, how she had been born and lived in a world that had ceased to exist, though its mementos were all about us; how her thimble had been fashioned as if in a magical grotto in the black mountain of time, by workmen dwarfed by remoteness, in a vanished workshop now no larger than the thimble itself and like it soon doomed, as if by geological pressures, to be crushed out of shape. O Lord, bless these poor paragraphs, that would do in their vile ignorance Your work of resurrection.

Although such fitly spoken words do not really tell us whether or not my father had a mantle that Eric wears they have, for me, become blessed goods.

Another letter from England, dated February 20, 1955, describes my father as a "presence" waiting at night for Eric and Joan to come back to their apartment. ("The birthday poem" was "March: A Birthday Poem," written in honor of Isabel's birth six weeks later and — on account of its directions for planting wheat, barley, and beans — my father's agricultural efforts, I thought. About the latter, it seems that I was mistaken.) "I have been thinking about my grandfather of late, but wasn't aware of his presence when I wrote the birthday poem, though, when we come into the apartment late at night, in the second before I flick on the light I can see him sitting there in the big armchair by the fire — or rather the cold fireplace."

When Eric returned to America in the following summer my father, presumably, came with him. It was July 9, to be exact, and a time when, ordinarily, I think well of myself. If I were a werewolf I would, almost certainly, be most dangerous then. Not really a werewolf — much as I admire wolves — I take liberties in July, when the summer solstice and my birthday are past, that could be taken at no other time. Bold enough to make decisions then, I have had my tonsils removed, decided to go back to a school I left in panic the previous year, accepted George's proposal of marriage, and six Julys later announced my pregnancy.

Although the temperature in the shade of the house was seventy degrees (and not really cool), it was a marked change from the hard-breathing summer heat that had greeted Eric and Joan when the *Britannia* docked in New York. Coming out of the house to hang a clothesline between one of Ann Gordon's pear trees and my mother's tree lilac, I heard a fall excitement in the screaming of the jays. The leaves of the poplars were rustling. And the breeze that stirred both bird and leaf seemed to have thrown the barn swallows high into the air where, rising and falling, they laughed like giddy children.

Looking away from the swallows, I noticed the speed with which the white rectangles of gauze skipped, one by one, into place on the clothesline. And, for a moment, I felt subdued as I was when, disappointed by one of my slow performances, my mother had said, "*Belle, you never finish anything.*" It had been true then and, to a shocking extent, still was. "Joan?"

"Yes?" A red plastic clothespin missed the clothesline and fell into the ragged grass.

"Do you think we're doing the right thing?"

"Yes. Don't you?"

"I'm not sure that this job is right for Eric."

"But you made the appointment for him." Retrieving the fallen clothespin, Joan fastened the last diaper.

"I did, didn't I? But I've made a lot of mistakes for which I'm sorry now."

"You needn't be, I'm sure."

"I'm glad." But Joan had hurried into the house to get Eric's breakfast and left me to consider — alone — the fact that it was too soon for me to have expected her to understand my uneasiness. That she had volunteered to stay with my mother, so that I might have a free day and meet the man who was going to be Eric's first employer, was enough reason to say, "I'm glad."

Later, when we were ready to leave, Joan said, "You both look very posh. Have a nice day."

"Thank you," I said. "We will."

Then Eric kissed her and, with much waving of hands, we left Joan smiling across the shaggy lawn.

"Take Twenty-two and stay off the skyway. Stay off the skyway." Eric and I would have felt more at home on the turnpike. But with George's advice echoing between us, we took the winding road that rolls like a runaway spool of gray ribbon from Reading to Monterey and Maxatawny and then, unexpectedly, turns left in Trexlertown to cross the corn fields and join Route 22 at Fogelsville.

Our leisurely progress caused us no anxiety. Eric's appointment was set for five and still five hours away. I can recall nothing that we said — only that we talked. I had

always — from that day in the hospital when it seemed as
though, magically, all that was wrong had righted itself —
talked as if everything that could not be said to George and
my parents had to be told to Eric. And it is to Eric's great
credit, I think, that he listened — was listening — while our
frequent encounters with earth-moving equipment on Route
22 covered his waterfall-blue car with burnt ocher dust. The
afternoon was hot, considering how cool the morning had
been, and we stopped for refreshments; so that when, at
last, we reached the Newark airport it was four o'clock.

We had only to remember George's directions. "Keep off
the skyway. Keep off the skyway."

"Is this the skyway, Mother? Shall I turn to the right?"

"Yes. Keep off the skyway." I could not say that I was
no more familiar with the "skyway" than I was with Communipaw Avenue where now we began to move forward
slowly behind a long line of trucks.

After an immeasurable time between trucks, we agreed
that a telephone call (to Mr. Wright) was obligatory and
Eric stopped to make it. We returned on the New Jersey
Turnpike by way of Camden, which is considerably farther
than taking Exit 6 to the Pennsylvania Turnpike, and Joan
was mowing the lawn when we drove into the yard at home.
George was reading a newspaper in the gathering gloom.
And since my mother seemed to be at ease in her bed, the
four of us sat down in the kitchen.

"Did Mr. Wright give you a job?" George asked.

"We didn't see Mr. Wright," Eric said.

"But where have you been?"

I remembered the fields of corn that grow between Mon-

terey and Maxatawny. I remembered the slow, feline turn-
ings of earth-moving equipment along Route 22 in New
Jersey and the incredible instant when, because of my wish
to avoid the skyway, Eric had turned into Communipaw
Avenue. And I remembered that there had been only two
other times in my life (Eric's birth and my first date with
George and Emmeline) when I could not stop laughing. "I
don't know, George," I said. "It was the funniest thing.
We were lost, I think."

"Lost? How could you get lost? I gave you directions."

"We know you did. But we didn't follow them."

After which Eric and I began to laugh again and Joan,
without laughing, said, "I wish I thought it was that funny."

But it was July and the kind of day in which I have no
regrets. After some time had passed Eric explained to
Joan and George that he had called Mr. Wright and made
another appointment for the next day. And — without a
word from anyone — it was understood that Eric would
make *this* trip alone.

ix

THE DAY was extraordinarily beautiful. It was October again and the sky's opalescent blue had been cleared of those things — excessive heat, high winds, and lightning — that my mother disapproved of in the weather. Given a second choice, she might have chosen to die when the ground was covered with crisp snow — so that her final ride to our family burial plot could have been made to the sound of sleigh bells. But she was smiling and pleased, presumably, with whatever it was that she saw in the moment of her death. Characteristic of her lighthearted moments, her smile was reminiscent of that delight small children show when, for the first time, they walk alone and free of helping hands. I took her hand in mine. There was no coldness in our touch, only an unmistakable coolness. Then I called George and, seeing that my mother was dead, he knelt with his clasped hands on the edge of her bed and began a very surprising prayer.

His words surprised me, certainly, and might have surprised my mother (who must have known from the start how difficult it was for me to be her daughter) even more. And so, instead of entering into George's prayer for me, I recalled the day, five months earlier, when Dr. Wentzel, after noticing how uneven her breathing was, lifted one of her eyelids and said, "She is dying, Belle. I don't know how long it will take."

Lilacs were in bloom — the burgundy ones she had planted close to the house and those pale lavender ones that were planted by another in a different time altogether — and while my mother slept, I watched them turning from side to side in the rain. May is not a time of dying and she, although dying, lived through the summer. And I like to think that she — long familiar with illness — was not afraid to die as my father, whose final illness was his first, had been afraid. Like him, however, she was concerned for me on account of the natural ebullience that from time to time had prompted Aunt Hester to say, "This child will be a disgrace to the whole family, if she lives long enough." It was as if, instead of the middle-aged woman I was, my parents still believed me to be the child I, at first, had been.

Now, his apology for my ebullience ended, George got up and said, "I never wanted to see your mother helpless, Belle. I never wanted to see her die."

"But we didn't see her die, George. And I'm glad we didn't." It seemed unfortunate, I thought, that George's work had kept him away from home all through the summer, so that he could not see how far from being helpless, while dying, my mother had been.

"Mom was a tough bird." The sharp edge of a meaning that had at first made both of us smile was gone. But even now, looking down, the word "beautiful" came to mind. There was no other word for the coin-bright face. Often, in the long months when we were alone, I had wondered whether or not my father believed in the legend of her beauty. Was it beyond his understanding — as it had been beyond mine? When the last (and oldest) of my eleven uncles said to me, after my mother's death, "She was a beauty, a real beauty," I was pleased as a child, reading one of the great fairy tales, is pleased to find that beauty, too, is one of the facts of life. But since my mother's beauty had faded before I was born and its remnant was so oddly Byzantine (or birdlike), it seemed — as the frail splendors of the East ever have been desired by men of the West and taken without understanding — that my father could not have appreciated it.

Like the Norseman of Bayard Taylor's "The Palm and the Pine," however, my father had wooed and won her without any difficulty:

> When Peter led the First Crusade,
> A Norseman wooed an Arab maid.

He loved her lithe and palmy grace,
And the dark beauty of her face:

She loved his cheeks, so ruddy fair,
His sunny eyes and yellow hair.

He called: she left her father's tent;
She followed wheresoe'er he went.

She left the palms of Palestine
To sit beneath the Norland pine.

She sang the musky Orient strains
Where Winter swept the snowy plains.

Their natures met like Night and Morn
What time the morning-star is born.

The child that from their meeting grew
Hung, like that star, between the two.

A long description of "the child that from their meeting
grew" follows and the poem's final couplets are:

But how he lived, and where, and when
It matters not to other men;

For, as a fountain disappears,
To gush again in later years,

So hidden blood may find the day,
When centuries have rolled away;

And fresher lives betray at last
The lineage of a far-off Past.

That nature, mixed of sun and snow
Repeats its ancient ebb and flow:

The children of the Palm and Pine
Renew their blended lives — in mine.

This poem, I thought, described my parents' relationship with me exactly. For almost fifty years I had "hung, like that star, between the two" and felt "the children of the Palm and Pine renew their blended lives — in mine." And after my father's death, my references to "The Palm and the Pine" became a conversational commonplace. Which is not to say that I, waiting for George to come home and feeling "the lineage of a far-off Past" in the bond that bound me to her really intended to imply that my mother was an Arab. And why it amused me, during the summer she was dying, to try to reconstruct verbally the long way her forebears had come to be a part of the emigration from Holland to Pennsylvania in the latter years of the eighteenth century, I cannot say. I doubt that my remarks amused anyone else. But of course I was the only one who was alone and otherwise unamused.

Certainly there was no reason for me to say that my mother, in our last summer together, had been helpless. Moreover, aside from a legend of her former beauty, there was little else that I really *knew* about her.

I remembered how my father, with the air of a conspirator, had said, "Depend upon it, Belle, I couldn't have found a better wife — than your mother."

Then, naturally and somewhat presumptuously, I assumed that his confession referred to the innumerable efforts on his behalf that I had observed: her trips into Reading to peddle a wagonload of eggs, butter, potatoes, apples, or whatever happened to have grown on the farm, caring for my grandmother during her dotage, feeding chickens and steers (not to mention mules and cows) in addition to the preparation of our meals, the custody of a horse and house, and last, but not the least interesting in my observations of them, were those cheerful attentions she gave to my father. Of these his footbaths were most memorable. But smaller services — the removal of his boots and putting on of shoes — were sufficiently strenuous to hold my attention so that my father, noticing that I was standing idly by, often said, "I can do this, Belle. But it gives your mother so much pleasure to do it. You wouldn't want me to deny that pleasure to her, would you?"

After which I invariably smiled because, indeed, it seemed that tying my father's shoelaces had given her pleasure.

Now, however, I doubted that this was so. Fifty-six years — the number of years my parents were married — is a very long time to take pleasure in tying another person's shoelaces. Her other services had ended with the sale of the farm and the progress of palsy.

Yet, although she had been less active in the last ten years of her life, there was no time to learn what now, seeing her dead, I wanted to know. After all, it was Aunt Anna's husband — not my father — who was moved to say, "Your mother was a beauty." My father, with whom on another occasion I had had a difference of opinion about a minor change in the appearance of his suburban house, said, "Beauty is a matter of opinion and what you may call beautiful may be *ugly* to someone else."

Shocking as this statement was, I had to agree that it was true. And since, in reality, I had never thought of my mother as "a beauty" — but on the other hand "ugly" enough to make a person run and hide sometimes — I wondered whether, or not, my father ever had considered her beautiful. It may be that she was "a beauty." In retrospect, however, it seems as if she expected — in the beginning of her marriage — the fact that she was both quick and loving to compensate for her lack of beauty. Or, sure of her beauty and carrying her love like a banner into my grandmother's house, had she found them less useful than her agility? And, angrily then, had she destroyed (beginning with the most fragile one) her gifts?

The truth was never quite clear to me, naturally. Little by little, therefore, I explained the mystery that I could not observe by setting her "beauty" in another time and place. And my father — in my fantasy — was always the crude "crusader" who, having wooed "an Arab maid," did not really love "the dark beauty of her face." Otherwise, I thought, my mother would have kept her beauty for him.

In any event it was good to remember now that my mother had lighthearted moments to the accompaniment of sleigh bells and singing and the dark-eyed laughter of her swarthy brothers and slender sisters. When visiting her brothers and sisters — not to mention the dozens of good-looking cousins they had given me — my mother's sudden gaiety frightened me. But there was no longer any need for me to be afraid; the summer of her helplessness was over. And when George got up from his knees I said, "She was the youngest of ten children and lived the longest. I'm glad."

"She was a wonderful woman and I'm going to miss her."

"She always liked you."

"I don't want to live with you — *without her.*"

Then, instead of saying that he was sorry to have said such a cruel thing, George went into the bathroom and closed the door. I could see him smiling there, as though the thought that he had loved my mother and now was free to leave us both was an invitation to spend the day in paradise. And since this would be my first free day in the two years that followed my father's death there was no need, certainly, to envy George his thoughts of freedom. This invitation to spend the day in paradise, whatever George thought, included me *and* my mother. "We're both free now," I said. "I've called the undertaker and he is on his way. Then we're going to town to buy new clothes for me."

What followed — after my mother's body had gone — was no ordinary shopping trip. My sense of freedom, after the morning's discovery, had been iced by an awareness of time as a palpable thing.

When George started the car, I smiled and thought of all the things that had to be done *now.* The heavy fluid of summer had become, with the reality of my mother's death, a solid that, having taken the form of a scroll, was suddenly unrolled in my hands — extended for one instant of awful certainty — and re-rolled in reverse so that the present was underneath the past.

This sense of being both young and happy again out-lasted the buying of black suede pumps, a white silk blouse, and a black suit. The ease with which these purchases had been made suggested my mother's presence. Everything, in fact, suggested my mother's presence. By what magic she could, with the hitching of her sorrel thoroughbred in the yard of a city hostelry, become a woman of the world instead of the dispirited wife of a sandhill farmer I never understood. Nature had given her the quick eye of the born brigand and to follow her on a tour of the stores was to be transported along the route of one of those camel caravans where the world's wealth could be ours without a doubt or haggle. Now, feeling this magic at work on my behalf, I said to Miss Good, "I need a hat."

Miss Good, whose hair, through magic of another sort, was the exact color of the furniture, edged a light blue chair around to face a table with mirrors. "Won't you put your parcels on the table, Mrs. Adams?"

"It should be a black hat. But color doesn't really matter. My suit had fuchsia lines in it. A fuchsia hat might be nice."

"Is it for dress — or casual wear?"

"It's for my mother's funeral."

"Oh, I am sorry. Did she have a long illness?"

"Yes, it was." "Siege" was my mother's word for all extended periods of discomfort. Curiously she who seemed to have lived entirely in the present — fearful of the future and forgetful of the past — had known this word from out of our beleaguered past and used it with all of the familiarity that the Moors of Malaga might have given to it in 1487. Now, unless I used the word, it might never be used again. "It was a long siege," I said.

"Painful?"

"Only for me. She didn't complain."

"Do you remember the hats I used to sell her?"

"I remember one she bought for me."

Plainly as if the photographic enlargement in its old-fashioned gilded frame had suddenly appeared in the air over Miss Good's head, I could see myself — short-legged and long-faced, at the age of seven — in a wide-crowned beaver hat, the enormous weight of which seemed to be hanging from a pair of flapping black wings. The eyes of the girl in the picture are big and clear and meet the eye of the camera with a calm that seems to belong in another world. There is a firmness in the set of the child's closed lips that, at this time, had caused her mother to speak of "stubbornness."

"I hope we can go quickly, don't you?" Miss Good said.

"I'm in no hurry — to go. Not that there's much reason for me to go on living — now."

"Why say that? Aren't you the mother of Eric Adams?"

"Yes."

"I think he's going to be famous, don't you?"

"Yes."

Twitching the chair a bit closer to my knees, Miss Good said, "Why don't you sit down? You must be very tired."

"I really can't sit down. It's been a long time since I've taken the time to look in a mirror."

"But you should have. We've sold you some beautiful hats."

"Like this one?" Lifting a fuchsia-colored beret from one of the hatstands in the alcove set aside for "originals," I said, "It's not *round*, is it?"

"No. It's not round." Although smiling, Miss Good shifted her weight from one foot to the other and sighed.

"I've had round hats and my head, you see, isn't round."

"I know. I've been selling hats to your mother ever since you were a little girl. Let's try these." Miss Good came forward with a black hat in each hand. "This is the only way to find out what we can wear. I know you need a large head size."

Her voice was a golden net, made in an instant from the air between us, and mine a rusty shield that I blushed to raise. "George says that I have my father's head. But we have an appointment with the undertaker — to make the arrangements. He's probably at home now." I waved one of my father's wide hands at the mound of parcels. "All are exactly what she would've bought for me — a black knit suit with fuchsia stripes, suede shoes that fit, and a blouse of real silk. Do you understand? I need a hat."

"I understand. Let's just try on these hats for size."

Suddenly aware of my reflection in the mirror behind the table where my packages lay, I sat down. "Forgive me," I said. "I'm not myself today."

It was a mistake to let Miss Good think of me as a mourner. And the hope of finding — in my own person — a beauty that had long ago become a legend in my mother's was absurd. Yet hope and mourning had become one on the day my mother, turning suddenly away from the mirror where she stood braiding her long hair, said, "You'll never look like me, Belle. You'll never be half as good-looking as I was." And so, supporting each other, both hope and sorrow for the little girl mirrored in my mother's flashing brown eyes that day had survived. Secretly that little girl had admired the little girl she saw when — bright-eyed and hopeful — she looked into the parlor mirror to see if, after all, she might be as pretty as her cousin Edwina. To know that her mother had no such hope for her was a great shock. The shock has been great enough, in fact, to have shattered her faith in mirrors. So that when Miss Good lifted one of the black hats — as though, all at once, it was a freshly baked cake — and held it above the middle-aged face in the mirror, I said, "I can't wear black. Let's try that red hat."

"Do you mean the fuchsia beret?"

"Yes."

"It's a *good* hat. Do you think it will be comfortable?"

"Yes."

"Wouldn't you like to try it on?"

"No. Thank you. The undertaker must be tired of waiting."

Then seeing how broadly Miss Good was smiling, I knew that my mother seemed close — momentarily — to her too.

$\mathcal{X}$

JOB'S DAUGHTER

AT THE LAST MOMENT, George decided to go to Philadelphia instead of taking me to New York, as he had, the night before, promised. The excitement of the longer drive with George was preferable to the shorter ride on the Pennsylvania railroad. And I was glad to be on the turnpike again. The broad paths of concrete and the sunshine on the trees — "scraggly trees," George called them — invariably revived my spirits to a point where memories that I ordinarily could not enjoy became enjoyable. There was the time, for example, when surveyors were setting their marks among the trees and those who watched them from the fields had called it "the fools' road" and said it would never be used. My father, usually pleased by new under-takings, had refused to look into the half-cleared right-of-way. "I'm well acquainted with stones," he said.

"Not these," I had begged. "They're taller than George and very frightening." Yet my father would not go to see them.

In the following winter, George sometimes took me, on Sundays at sundown, to see the giant boulders in the clearing and feel the glacial cold that had survived a dozen millenniums in the sun. With a hand on the slate-gray flank of one of the stone behemoths, I said, "Why didn't the road turn out for them? How will they move them?"

"Dynamite."

Although long since broken and buried under the turn-pike, the rocks were still whole in my mind — a monument to the man who dared to set the dynamite and, daring, died with the stones. Two months later, on a summer's job with the road-builders, George had been dehydrated. He always pointed, in passing, to the exact spot.

Afterward, we talked about my father whose memory, now that he was dead, filled my thoughts with a kind of wonder that was close to shock. If, when it was too late, I discovered that my husband too was more like Job than I ever suspected, I had no idea what might happen; for this belated realization that I had not really understood my father and was frequently unkind to him when I should have been most kind had disturbed me — surprisingly.

"But why wouldn't he come with us to look at those pieces of a mountain?"

"Eric understood his grandfather," George said. "Ask him."

Inclined to measure Eric's understanding of all things by my own, I said, "Eric didn't laugh when Grampy called himself another Job, did he?"

"No. He understood his grandfather."

"It's nice to think someone did."

When Eric came back from his honeymoon to find his grandfather dead he had, in fact, given me a cool look and said, "I always thought of him as a benevolent man."

At the moment, I had not known whether to laugh because Eric sounded so incredibly adult, or cry because I suddenly felt like a lost child. "He *was* a patient man and generous to a fault, as he used to say. Why did we always laugh when he said it?" Since Eric had ventured no explanation, I thought the explanation probably was due to the fact that my father rarely looked either patient or poor. In the weeks following his funeral, however, his heartbreaking cough echoed in the house and once, driving home from the station with George, I *saw* him. The vision hurried along, ahead of us, on the edge of the dusty road — younger than the man I knew and marked, plainly, by sufferings of a spiritual nature. And it was the vision, rather than the man, I remembered now.

"Your father was a handsome man." As he watched the road with partly closed eyes, George's profile was like George Washington's.

To have contradicted him would have been unthinkable

and yet contradiction was, I imagined, what he needed to support the advantage gained by the conversational gambit just used. "Yes, my father had many admirers — especially among the women."

"He could have been one of the best judges our county ever had."

"But aren't you glad he wasn't a judge?" The road had climbed a hill and was running along the side of it so that I could look across the treetops to a plain where I suspected Paoli of being. "Life with us being what it was, George."

This new insight into the character of my father had forced me to make another inventory of George's virtues and my own. And, naturally, I had been shaken to find a good deal of chaff among the wheat. But even before I had come to a recognition of the need for self-appraisal, George said, "Belle, you know you have only one virtue." Then, without waiting for me to ask its name, he said, "Loyalty." It was a pleasant virtue, I thought (although not one of the greatest), and I accepted it with gladness and the hope of adding others later. With all of the deadly sins to confess and all of the Christian virtues to be cultivated, my future would be busy, if not bright. There was no need, really, to make a list of George's spiritual assets. It was better to say, simply, that he had no faults — habits, perhaps, that I would have broken, but no faults. And, among the latter, the only truly bad one was his way of saying, "I hate everybody."

The words seemed to bubble from an unfailing spring of inner delight. Sometimes, I felt as though the words had always been a part of his conversation. Yet I knew very well when the habit had taken hold of George.

Loitering at the dinner table with Eric and Joan, I had been talking about Goldie and the way I found him dead in a neighbor's corn field. At home again, we had buried the dog on a terrace near the house and my father, cupping the end of a shovel handle in the palm of his hand, said, "Don't let your grief unhinge your mind, Belle." Eric and his grandfather exchanged smiles then. And I forgave them because, naturally, they could not know how I felt.

Then my mother, who had not smiled, said, "We'll never have a dog like Goldie. He was the nicest dog I ever saw." Remembering now how the four of them had stood together in the shadow of the house on that humid July afternoon, I wondered if anything had ever been quite the same again. But five years had passed. Now Eric was engaged and Joan had come to visit.

"Joan, I wish you could have seen him. His hair was the color of moonlight and five inches long." My eyes prickled with tears. "I'm glad he died for love — fighting a beagle twice his weight."

It was at this point that George, who had been watching Joan all the while, said, "I hate everybody."

Joan laughed, letting her voice rise in a lovely arietta, and Eric blushed. I, too, had smiled, looking across the old table at Joan — dear, lovely Joan. "How nice it must be to be so lovely that hatred amuses you?" Still talking to myself while George related a humorous episode from his own "struggle for existence," I said, "Now I am a mother-in-law. What's more, I don't really like being a mother-in-law. But if George hadn't said what he just did, I might have gone on without knowing the difference between being Eric's mother and Joan's mother-in-law. It would have been better not to know — ever so much better. The sensation of falling in a dream always ends with the relief of waking up, but from the sensations of a mother-in-law there would be no awakening."

George, tired of saying, "I hate everybody," then left the table. And I, seeing that my father looked more pale than usual, said, "I guess he can't help saying it, or being the way he is."

"But it worries me, Belle."

At this, I laughed. So old and ill, he surely had not expected me to believe him capable of a real concern for anyone else. And yet his face, a mask of anxiety, held no answering gleam of amusement. He *was* worried — just as, although neither old nor ill, I was worried now — by George. Patience, however, had upheld my father while I, having nothing but "loyalty" to depend on, often wondered what to do next. There was, after all, a chance that I might grow more patient and I devoutly hoped it might be soon. With this hope in mind, I had begun to watch television and, quite accidentally, discovered a program called "Tic Tac Dough."

Alone at the time of the discovery, I tried to share it with George on the drive to Philadelphia. The hugely smiling although defeated players and the way Mr. Mooney said, "You've been a delightful contestant" suggested degrees of patience that Job himself had never attained. I was enthralled by the regularly recurring spectacle of grown people behaving like happy children. But George said, "Quiz programs make me nervous."

"Isn't that what they're supposed to do, George? Please come along and ask for an interview. You know so much more than I do."

"I wouldn't go on that program for a million dollars." George's well-boned jaw indicated that this was his final word. "But *you* have my blessing."

"Oh, thank you." I began looking for the Philadelphia exit. Later I might be angry, or vaguely ill; but before that happened, I would be on the train. "Do you think Mr. Harker will know why I want to be a contestant?"

"Why do you?"

"I don't know exactly. For one thing, I'm curious about the way they choose contestants and I want to see whether or not I'll be one of them."

"I don't care if you aren't one of them."

"Why?"

"Don't forget, we're repulsive."

"Perhaps that is what I want to know — how repulsive I am. I haven't seen any really repulsive people playing Tic Tac Dough. Most of them behave so well they hardly seem to be real."

"They aren't real. You know damn well they're not."

"But they are, George. Last week's big winner had ten children."

"All right. That's what I'm trying to tell you. They aren't real. Wasn't one kid enough for me?"

"Yes. Eric was." As music charms the angry breast, the thought of our only child invariably calmed us. Sometimes, the magic name worked more slowly than at other times. This time, the change came at once, showing itself in a full minute of silence.

Then, in the fine baritone voice he held in reserve for magical moments, George said, "How much money did this Spaniard win?"

"He was from Texas and I don't know the amount of money. He was *very* interesting, Mr. Mooney said."

"This Mr. Harker, who is he?"

"The producer of the show — the man who picks the contestants."

Whereupon George's jowl rounded with whatever it was that made him say, "I hate everybody." And he said, "I *hate* Mr. Harker, don't I?"

On the platform outside of the North Broad Street Station, I found a companion for the train ride to New York, a lanky widow and the kind of woman that, without the joined virtues of George and my father to protect me from my own lack of virtue, I might have been. The woman had so much to say on such a variety of subjects that afterward I wondered what she did on those rare occasions when her fellow traveler was equally well-informed. At any rate, the mood set by our one-sided conversation was a brave one and my cab driver sustained it from the Pennsylvania Station to the address on the square envelope in my hand.

"Now slide to the door and put both feet on the curb," he said.

I did as I was told and backed away from the taxi. "Oh, thank you," I said. "I'd never have escaped without your directions."

Grinning and waving his right hand at me, the man nosed the cab back into the northbound traffic while a dime that he had given me slipped between my fingers and ran away on the pavement in the path of one of those remarkable middle-aged men who can wear a checked suit and carry a cane without looking effete. It was extremely nice, I thought, that he was able to see the small coin in flight and return it to me so promptly — his hat and cane notwithstanding. I thanked him and looking up at the granite-faced building, matched the number above its wide glass door with the number on the envelope in my hand and took a deep breath. The air of Madison Avenue was uncommonly clean and cool, I thought. Then, taking another deep breath, I opened the wide glass door and found myself instantly in a gray-green world where the air was somewhat less clean and cool and my specific gravity seemed to increase with every step.

A short man, waiting at the top of the stairs, made me realize that this gray-green world where we stood was not, after all, the familiar one. To my polite good morning and a request to be taken to the top floor, he said, "Nobody's there."

"But I have an appointment with Mr. Harker."

"Lady, he's gone to England. He was in here yesterday with a bunch of people. You know?"

"Does this sort of thing happen very often?"

Holding his head at a thoughtful angle, the man said, "No."

"May I wait?" I smiled at the small chair beside the wall. "On your chair?"

He said nothing. When I was seated, however, he said, "I'll go in here."

Pacing the square cove made by the two elevator shafts and a big desk, he turned the morning's collection of letters so often that I thought how George would have hated the little chair and the small man and — most of all — the enclosure behind the big desk. But George, having given me his blessing, was free now to walk all the way to Independence Square. By this time, he would be eating a sandwich in one of those narrow places where the proprietor's newspaper can be shuffled while keeping an eye on the people in the street. To see George now in my imagination, his face turned to the restaurant window and expectation in every line of his long body, made it possible for me to forgive many, if not quite all, of the times he had worried me by saying, "I hate everybody."

"Is there nobody to verify my appointment?"

"Down the street on the corner, there's a drugstore — if you want to make a call." His face widened the way George's sometimes did.

"I'm Mrs. George Adams, if anyone should ask. I'll be back." And I was. After looking into a telephone directory where I found none of the names I wanted, I waited now with my back to the desk, at the greatest possible distance from its guardian. The people who came and went on the stairs seemed to be, if not quite transparent, less dense than people ordinarily are. I weighed them, one by one, in my mind and said, "No, not this one." Yet I believed that the glass doors, turning and returning between the stairs and the sunny pavement, would admit someone capable of saving me from the shame of having to tell George that my appointment with Mr. Harker had been no more real than the people who played Tic Tac Dough. Out of necessity my thoughts turned back to moments of shame I had survived. With these remembrances, I could hear my father's voice. The face was less clear than his words. But my impression was that his familiar admonition had been spoken with a certain equally well-known smile. "We must exercise a little patience, Belle. These things will not last forever."

As a matter of fact, my dismay was turned to joy almost immediately, for there, at last, was a *real* person among the ascending and descending wraiths. He was frowning and a little out of breath when he stopped at the top of the stairs to explain his tardiness.

Rising briskly, the elevator took us to the top floor. Two other candidates for Tic Tac Dough had emerged from the shadows and were now trotting along a breezy labyrinth at the young man's heels. "Go in, please, and sit down. I'll see you in a moment."

Putting my hat and eyeglasses on the table, I took a blurred view of my associates. It was the woman who said, "I guess we are here for the same reason."

The man said, "I guess *so*."

Whatever I might have said to the contrary — and it almost certainly would have been to the contrary — was forestalled by a prompt reappearance of the young man. I followed him into another, smaller room where, for the first time, he looked directly at me. Both the dark green shirt and the way he carried his shoulders suggested El Greco's Saint Andrew. "My name is Sharadin," he said, closing the door. "Can you bear this cold and dismal place for a little while?"

"It's very comfortable, I think." And the way Mr. Sharadin circled his half of the room, touching one thing after another — files, desk, Venetian blind — with tentative fingers, delighted me.

Seated finally, he took a two-handed grip on the written

results of my first interview. "You say here that curiosity brings you here."

"Yes." Disarming as this young man was, I could not confess that I had come because I felt like a lost child at home — with my parents dead and Eric married and George hating everybody. At any rate Mr. Sharadin looked as though he knew exactly how I felt.

"And you have a master's degree?"

"Yes."

"What have you done with it?"

"Nothing. Really."

"Nothing?" Incredulity lifted his eyebrows and parted his lips.

Seeing how small and perfectly matched his teeth were, I thought of the girl who had asked to "try" my father's teeth to see if they were his very own. My father's pleasure in this incident had lasted, unabated, until his death at ninety and now, in a flash of hindsight, I could see how it might have been one of the turning points in his long life and a first step toward becoming "another Job." Certainly it had made a satisfactory relationship with me — a daughter whose upper lateral incisors were set askew — more difficult than it should have been. And when I was faced, at sixteen, with George's enormously uneven grinders, sympathy had bound us together — irreparably. "I was married that year," I said.

Mr. Sharadin looked down, then, at the paper on which I had made a list of the most interesting events in my life and nodded. "You were a teacher?"

"No, my husband teaches and I've been trying to learn."

"Have you learned?"

"I find it very difficult to concentrate on any one thing." Noticing that Mr. Sharadin had stopped smiling, I said, "I guess I'm just another happy amateur."

"A happy *amateur?*"

"Yes, *I* think I'm a *happy* amateur," I said, somewhat crossly.

"That's interesting," he said. "We'll call you in about two weeks, if you think you can arrange to be here then."

When we met again, Mr. Sharadin was marshaling his forces at the entrance to Studio B in the RCA Building. He had aged a good deal, I thought, in the sixteen days since our interview and his outward resemblance to the Saint Andrew by El Greco was gone. Now he more nearly resembled a merry-andrew who, having found the loaves and fishes, had taken his portion in the form of caviar and toast. "I was lost," I said, breathing fast. "Downstairs in the subway."

His eyes widened a little, but his smile implied that it could have happened to anybody. "Come and meet the other contestants. Mr. Shelley, our current champion, and Mrs. Gordon will go on first. Mr. Nace and Mr. Perwein are three and four. You'll be five."

Two hours remained before the program was scheduled to begin — two hours in which we, after the coolest of greetings, began to talk to one another in the uninhibited way of children on a picnic. "My being here is just a gag." Mr. Perwein moved his hands and his head with so much animation that the word Etruscan came to mind. "But my boss isn't laughing anymore."

"He needs you. Isn't that nice?" I said.

"This will probably be one of the most wonderful days in all of our lives." Mr. Perwein could, almost certainly, have traced his descent from a funeral dancer of Etruria and seemed even now to be feeling like a champion. "It will be very much like having a baby, I imagine," he said.

After which Mr. Sharadin began to give us our final instructions and I shifted the contents of my handbag to find the tiny box with "Nerves" written largely on its side.

"This is not a dramatic show," Mr. Sharadin was saying. "If you feel tense, take a deep breath and hold it. If you feel like talking on camera, talk. If you feel like hitting someone, wait until after the program. Now, are there any questions?"

Mr. Perwein raised a long, lean hand. "May I have a ladies' watch to console me?"

"Yes."

Mr. Schultz raised his hand next. "What are the watches worth?"

The question was so obviously improper that Mr. Sharadin blushed and was, for a moment, speechless.

"We brought nothing into this world and we'll take nothing out." This turn of thought, expressed by Mr. Perwein, struck me who had brought George's blessing, a return fare to Birdsboro, and a sum of money that was now so completely spent that I would have to borrow unless I won at Tic Tac Dough, to pay my hotel bill, as a falsity of the first magnitude.

Mr. Sharadin, however, raised both hands in a kind of

benediction as though the words had been rehearsed for use in this very spot. "Precisely," he said.

Mr. Schulz grinned and rubbed his hands together, but his eyes were angry. "Thank you," he said.

No one else seemed to care.

In conclusion, Mr. Sharadin said, "You're all beautiful. Fat and thin, tall or short, you are here because of your good looks, or interesting personalities. Some of you were awfully quiet in rehearsal. Both Mr. Shelley and Mrs. Adams looked rather too stoical. Be casual. Smile. This is *not* Shakespeare. *Have fun.*" Whereupon he eased himself from the high stool on which he had been sitting and disappeared in the direction of the studio audience.

It was just one minute short of high noon — too late for asking questions and too early for answering them. It was a time intended, especially, for taking a deep breath and holding it and, having swallowed one of the tablets from the little white box, I was beginning to inhale when Mr. Shelley, instead of doing what he might have been doing preparatory to the defense of his championship, said, "You remind me of someone."

"Do I?" Oddly enough, Mr. Shelley was rather like George.

"Yes." His wide lips met self-consciously over the whispered name. "She was our pastor's wife."

"I'm not related to anybody in the ministry. None of my folks ever were." It struck me as a remarkable thing too, considering how Biblical their characters were. "I don't know why."

"I can scarcely believe you aren't related to her."

"I'm sorry." I laughed and held out my right hand. And I was truly sorry although — with five thousand dollars — Mr. Shelley needed no sympathy nor, indeed, was *that* what he wanted from me — if he *was* like George. "Play carefully now," I said.

Then, with a stoical smile, Mr. Shelley dropped my hand and, a short time later, his championship. Mrs. Gordon lost her winnings to Mr. Nace who decided against risking them in further play, so that Mr. Perwein succeeded to the championship automatically and I became his challenger immediately. There had been time enough, however, for me to think of George. "This is one of the last things I ever expected you to do," he had said. "It scares me."

"It scares me, too. But those people look so nice and their smiles, when they lose what they've already won, are enough to make one wonder. Anyway, it would be wonderful if we should happen to win a little money. Not that I really expect to be a champion. But wouldn't it be a wonderful thing, George?"

There had been no affirmation from George, only the words "You have my blessing." And the sadness that lined his face was visible now, making the playing board, ordinarily so gay with familiar categories, a dour threat. In the lower center box, which was not the box Mr. Sharadin advised all challenging contestants to enter, I saw the words "Comic Strips." "Comic Strips," I said.

The first question, luckily, asked me to name one of my favorite characters. My reply, therefore, was both proper and prompt and it seemed, as the circular sign of success flashed into the lower center box, that I might be a winner after all. Mr. Perwein's X in the upper left-hand corner was not going to keep me from having fun. The little pains were gone from my chest. Spirits, both benevolent and gay, seemed to be rubbing elbows in the outer darkness. My face, in the monitor, was smiling brightly.

Mr. Perwein missed his next question and I said, "I'll take Comic Strips in the center box."

"This will be a more difficult question. I'll give you extra time if you need it." Mr. Mooney was solemn and solicitous. "I'll give you the names of two comic strips. You tell us who created them. 'Dick Tracy' and 'Little Orphan Annie.'"

" 'Dick Tracy' was created by Chester Gould." I recalled Eric's gallery of comic-strip characters and, knowing that Little Orphan Annie was not among them, could think of nothing else. The collection of cartoons, like all of Eric's undertakings, had been both ambitious and heartwarming. In one short season, the walls of his room had bloomed with drawings all carefully signed: "For Eric Adams, with my very best wishes." Then, in another season, all but one of them disappeared. Madame Lynx and Steve Canyon had hung above the gray chest of drawers until *Self-portrait*, by Eric's wife, outranked them. At the same time, Soglow's Little King abdicated in favor of Joan's photograph. Eventually, all of the drawings had gone to the attic — with the exception, of course, of Thurber's *Dog*, who still made conversation in the living room.

"Your time is up, Mrs. Adams. I'll have to call for your answer."

"I should know because my husband always read 'Little Orphan Annie' to me. When we were newly married, that is."

"Now he'll know you weren't listening. I'm awfully sorry."

I smiled to show that Mr. Mooney need not feel too awfully sorry for me. "I don't know why I didn't listen to my husband."

Whereupon Mr. Perwein set his mark in the lower right-hand corner of the board so that I had to take Pot Luck in the center box.

"To keep him from scoring diagonally and winning the game, here is your question: 'The theory that energy exists in space independent of matter and is an entity made up of definite units or particles called quanta was first advanced in 1901. In 1918, the German physicist who advanced this theory received a Nobel prize. Who was he?' "

My father had never said that Lot's wife, looking back to her home town and seeing it a shambles, might have *wanted* to become a pillar of salt. But now, with a choice between her fate and saying, "I don't know," *again*, I would have chosen the fate of Lot's wife. Having no choice, I said, "I really don't know."

"Would you like to take a wild guess?" Mr. Mooney was radiating both quanta and goodwill. "I'll tell you when your time is up."

"I'll say it was Charles Barkla."

"Max Planck was the name given me. I'm *awfully* sorry."

After the commercial, Mr. Perwein asked for a question on Latin America and won a third corner of the board.

The center box, due to my former failings, remained empty. "I'll try spelling," I said.

"Another question in the difficult center box?" Mr. Mooney raised his eyebrows and laughed.

"I've a one-track mind," I said.

Then, holding the question at arm's length, Mr. Mooney began to read. "A figure, or design, depressed below the surface of the material and having the normal elevations of the design hollowed out, so that an impression from the design yields an image in relief is called *intaglio*. Spell *intaglio*."

Although my return to familiar ground was too late to be of any real value, I felt better after spelling *intaglio*. It was an exciting word, the meaning of which I could feel in my bones. Feeling it now, I heard Mr. Perwein answer the question that, by giving him three X's in a row, finished the game. "I'm glad you won," I said. Then, seeing how Mr. Schultz was biting his lip, I said, "We'll be watching you tomorrow. And don't go into that center box at all, if you can avoid it."

"Mrs. Adams showed great courage and very poor judgment." Mr. Sharadin's face was foreshortened by sudden laughter.

If Mr. Sharadin had looked either disappointed, or "stoical," I might have begun to cry. It seemed as if George's spirit had shifted us all around — our bodies imperceptibly and our minds a great deal — so that, having gone to the trouble of saying the right things in their backstage small talk, these men now were on the verge of saying, "I hate everybody." And four men saying, "I hate everybody" might be very frightening indeed. "I'll have to hurry home," I said. "May I take my prize along?"

"Yes, you can get your watch at the office now."

Looking up into the young and lightly freckled face, I wondered how well he understood the special kind of loneliness that drove grown people to test themselves in this excruciating blend of primitive puberty rite and the Spanish Inquisition. "Thank you," I said. "Thanks for everything."

"Mrs. Adams, you were lovely." Repeating the words, slowly and carefully, as though he thought I might not remember or, worse, had failed to hear them the first time, he grinned. "You were lovely."

After a taxi had brought me safely away from the place where a party of youngsters, who had seen the show, started to heckle me, I was startled to find Mr. Sharadin and Mr. Mooney waiting on the narrow runway above the polished stairs where I had waited, so long ago, with the elevator man. But even more unexpected than the sight of them there was Mr. Mooney's offhand reference to "Evening Tic Tac Dough." "We're beginning it in September and would like you to be one of the first contestants. Can you be here?"

"No. I really couldn't." To have been lonely, or lovely, was not the same as *being* lonely and lovely. My "curiosity" had been satisfied, but an explanation of the intuitive process by which this satisfaction of mind was accomplished would have taken more time than I had. "I can't seem to remember things anymore," I said.

"Your test indicated no loss of memory."

"It has been nice — is nice here."

Later, when the elevator had taken us to the top floor and Mr. Sharadin gave me the prize watch, he looked a little tired, I thought. "Take care now," I said.

"I will. You do the same." He grinned again, but the line of his small, evenly matched teeth was blurred and faded quickly away. In fact, when I turned my head, Mr. Sharadin, too, was gone.

Now where Mr. Sharadin had so lately been, a very short man with a heart-shaped face was standing. "Did you ring?" he said in a peevish way that implied I was the sort of woman who spent too much of her time loitering in the vicinity of elevator shafts.

"Mr. Sharadin rang."

Then with his thumb on the buzzer, he repeated a line that, although oddly at variance with his action, was a familiar saying I had missed hearing since my father's death. "All it takes is a little patience."

"Yes, I know." If the elevator man had not appeared just then, I might have said, "I'm another Job — Job's daughter — that is."

$$xi$$

A PREDISPOSITION TO ENCHANTMENT

WE LEFT the little stone house where my grandmother was, as Mrs. Baker said, "sticking it well," and started to walk down the lane — Mrs. Baker, who lived on the next farm, her grandson Ivan, and I. I was four years old, Ivan three, and Mrs. Baker about sixty.

Elated by the unexpected arrival of two guests in the middle of a dull August morning, I hadn't heard Mrs. Baker refer to my grandmother as "the old thing" who, her great age and many infirmities notwithstanding, was "sticking it well." She made the remark to my mother, who carried the daily burden of my grandmother's care, and it was probably meant to have a cheering effect. But my father, coming into the house just then, was greatly depressed by it and, in fact, remembered Mrs. Baker's words to the end of his own long life without ever believing, I suspect, that kindness of a sort had prompted her to say them. In practically the same breath, Mrs. Baker said something that I have never forgotten.

As I left the house with Ivan and his grandmother, it was my plan, and my mother's wish, that I go with them to the end of our land — a thousand feet or so — and come back after seeing them cross the imaginary line where our land became theirs. Actually, the path we followed was not a lane at all but a public road on which the doctor's buggy, my father's mule team, and all of our neighbors traveled. It was a lovely place to walk barefooted because of the warm patches of sand that lay between the wagon tracks and the ragged edge of the meadow, where wild sunflowers and fox grapes grew. And the prospect of walking there with Ivan and his grandmother, although neither of them seemed to have anything to say to me, was delightful. Delight, indeed, carried me along, so that my feet scarcely touched the sharp stones that a recent thundershower had uncovered. For in addition to the familiar pleasures of the road, I felt the peculiar buoyancy of a person who is for the first time performing an important social obligation alone. More than an obligation, my progress with Ivan and his grandmother was a privilege indicative of the love my parents had for me. So that when we moved into the shade of the first of the two pairs of Spanish cherry trees that grew below the barn and, without preamble, Mrs. Baker told me to go home, I couldn't believe my ears. To leave our guests behind the barn was not my mother's wish, nor was it mine. Separation at this point was a breach of etiquette. We invariably walked with those who came calling on foot to a suitable turning point: a crossroad, a fork in the road, or (as my present plan was) to our property line. Any other course of action was unthinkable.

I must have turned to Ivan for help. At any rate, my memory of that morning includes a bright vignette of Ivan's face — a small, beautiful-boy face so expressive of well-considered diplomacy that its connection with the body of a three-year-old child seemed to me, even then, to have something of the supernatural in it.

Together, the old woman's words and the little boy's silence were so much like the things of which my dreams were made that I skipped a few steps down the road, just to make sure that I was not dreaming. Consequently, Ivan's grandmother stamped her foot and said, "You go home right now. We don't want you to *follow* us."

Mrs. Baker's use of the word "follow" changed my amazement to anger, for in my mind we were walking together, as equals. But instead of arguing this matter with Mrs. Baker I ran back to the house — where my parents, strangely enough, seemed to be waiting for me — and said, "Mrs. Baker chased me home — like a *dog*." And I showed them how she had stamped her foot.

My mother seemed to be too busy for words. But she smiled when my father said, "You must make allowances for Mrs. Baker. She is a grandmother. Belle, it's a terrible thing to be a grandmother."

"Is that why she stamped her foot at me?"

"No. She probably smelled the fox grapes and didn't want you to see her picking them."

By retracing my steps, I could have looked down the road from a vantage point behind the barn and watched Ivan's grandmother filling her floor-length apron with grapes. But the fondness I now feel for fox grapes was undeveloped at that time, and I remained indoors.

In contrast with my own interpretation of the incident, which was that Mrs. Baker, knowing how sincerely I admired Ivan, had discouraged my sociability in order to avert an untimely marriage, my father's explanation of the incident was a great comfort to me. But this does not mean that Mrs. Baker's influence ended here. When she stamped her foot, she changed me so that I was never quite the same again. Even now, when we call upon friends and my husband says, "We must go home now," and our hostess asks *why* we must leave so soon, he says, "Belle is afraid you will tell her to go home." It seldom is necessary for him to explain, and while I wait at the front door everyone begins to laugh — as though my husband had told a very funny joke.

Home is still my grandmother's house. Although I have lived in many other houses, I belong to my grandmother's house. And I am not happy away from it. Ivan, too, lives in the house to which his grandmother returned him without my help on that August morning when I was four and he was three. The houses that used to belong to our grandmothers — his so fierce and mine so feeble — and the lovely road that connects them now are ours. Rumors to the effect that this road will be macadamized start, but nothing comes of them. The road has not changed and we have grown old without really changing. Only the cherry trees, whose overripe fruit used to fall on the road and scent the air with wine, are gone.

On the upper side of the house, the sandy road sidles into an "improved" road that takes us to the shopping center, our church, and, once or twice a year, out of Pennsylvania into the stream of northbound traffic that flows at sundown along Boston's North Shore. There, in a very old clapboard house, we find our son, Eric, and his wife and four children waiting for us. The house invariably has a festive air, and after dinner I settle into a comfortable chair — without a thought of Mrs. Baker and the occasion upon which my father said, "It's a terrible thing to be a grandmother."

Recently, however, on the second day of our stay in Massachusetts — a visit that had begun, and continued, in a fine November drizzle — I was unexpectedly reminded of her.

Sitting in my favorite chair while the raindrops ran together on the window panes, it seemed to me — as it did to Edward Gibbon two hundred years earlier — that, all things considered, my life had been a very fortunate one. Eric's wife had turned the noon meal into a delectable feast, and Jonathan, our second grandson, seemed to have enjoyed it as much as I did.

After the noon meal, Eric and his wife and I, with Hans,

the elder of their sons, had gone into the backyard to plant the dogwood trees that Eric had asked us to bring from our woods. While we planted them, the drizzle turned to rain, and by the time we finished, our clothes were wet. My spirit, however, was undampened. And I felt, when we came back to the house, the curious buoyancy that once, on an August morning when I was four years old, had carried me around the corner of my grandfather's barn and into the shade of a Spanish cherry tree. So that when Eric, after getting into dry clothes, asked me if I thought he might catch a cold, I said, "No. Why should you?" At first, his worry puzzled me; then I realized that to Eric, whose childhood was a time of colds, my presence suggests chills and high fevers. And although he has been away from our home long enough to have lost this unhappy association, it persists. Later, seeing him come into the living room with a thermometer under his tongue, I smiled. It was much too soon, I thought, for him to be feeling the effects of the rain — or my presence.

Nevertheless, the air surrounding my chair had changed, and the room, usually bright with sunshine, moonlight, or the reflected glow of street lamps, was dark. At this point, my husband announced his need of a nap and Hans went into the library to play with his electric train and Eric, the thermometer still under his tongue, set out to find his wife, who was upstairs with the baby. Aside from the song that Hans was improvising while he played with the train, the house was completely still when Isabel, who was making lists of words that rhyme and using the coffee table as a desk, said, "I hate the way Hans sings."

Though unexpected, Isabel's announcement was familiar to me, in the way that half-remembered faces, or bits of poetry, are familiar. In my grandmother's house, there were many taboos, but it always was permissible to hate singing. So, in loving memory of the child who used to sing in my grandmother's house and never knew why her mother said, "Don't *sing*, child. You'll cry before supper," I decided not to tell Isabel that in my opinion she is, in respect to singing, like me, and therefore ungifted. Hans's voice was true, with a bell-like clarity that almost certainly should have suggested to Isabel that her words were rooted in envy. Yet her silence in the face of my laughter irritated me. Perhaps I wanted her to say, "Don't you hate to hear him sing, Mom-mom?" so that I might have said how much I liked to hear Hans sing. Pretending to be surprised, therefore, I said, "Isabel, you don't mean it."

Both the words and my pretended surprise were a trick used by my favorite aunt to correct those extravagances of speech to which, at Isabel's age, I was inclined. But Isabel went on with her writing and said nothing — as if, indeed, she hadn't heard my exclamation of disbelief. And in what I imagined to be a perfect imitation of my aunt's voice, I repeated, "Isabel, you don't mean it."

Then, sighing audibly into the mass of discarded notebook paper that lay on the table between us, she said, "Yes, I do."

Foolishly, I had forgotten the awful clarity of the human mind at the age of six.

A moment later I saw Jonathan run from the kitchen with a bottle of ginger ale in his arms. And, since he was at that time the first two-year-old I had ever seen with a full quart of Canada Dry in his possession, I turned my attention to him.

In a little while, after taking a long draught from the bottle, which he set at my feet, he came to my chair and, slipping a hand behind my left shoulder, prodded me gently. It may be that with this gesture he was offering both himself and the bottle to me. In retrospect, however, it seems more likely that Jonathan meant to say that he wanted to sit in the chair — enjoying his bottle — while I joined the other adults upstairs. But the prodding was so soon done that before I could speak he was gone — running in a circle he had measured to include the bottle, my feet, and the chair.

Watching him, I thought of my father, for Jonathan has the long spine and short, well-muscled legs that supported my father's reputation as a "strong man." Once, in a moment of expressed sympathy comparable to his explanation of my sudden separation from Mrs. Baker and Ivan, he had told me, "My nickname, when I was young, was The Bull." And it was easy to see that he had not entirely recovered from the shock of learning that someone he knew had disliked him enough to feel the suitability of this nickname. Certainly it had not occurred to him that he might have accepted this title as a compliment. In fact, my father's attempts at guessing what went on in the minds of other people were seldom successful.

Yet Jonathan now seemed to have read my thoughts. With lowered head and both arms lifted, as though they were horns, he ran to my chair and struck my upper left side. A second blow, aimed in the same direction, was

averted by the abrupt extension of my left arm. Whereupon Jonathan dropped his arms and, without raising his
head, backed away to the circumference of the circle that
he seemed to see and, standing there, said, "Go home, go
home, go home."

Surprised as I had been when Mrs. Baker stamped her
foot and sent me home, it seemed momentarily as if those
long and happy years of my life when — outwardly, at least
— I was not a dog, had never been. It was as if the magic
circle within which, in my mind's eye, my humanity lies
had closed and left me outside, waiting alone for this dark
November day to end.

There have been other times when, in one of these
strange reversals of a happy mood, I have been told to
go home. Without exception, I have gone quietly and
quickly. There is no word, really, to say at such times. At
any rate, there is nothing for me to say. I am speechless.
It is as though the sound of the words cast a spell.

More accurately, these words remind me of the possibility
that a spell has been cast. For enchantment, per se, is not
easy to detect and after its discovery, requires a persistent
use of the contradictory magic for its undoing. Whether
my own enchantment began with Mrs. Baker or with an
incident that happened before I was born, I do not know.
Thinking of it after many years, I believe it was the latter,
and that Mrs. Baker was only a witch who took advantage
of my susceptibility. Locally, the incident is spoken of as
"the time the lightning struck in the Plow Hotel." Of the
three young men who stood at that time on the hotel
porch, two were killed. But it is the third man that I see,
getting up from the porch floor and glaring in all directions

because he thought that his friends, in a fit of rowdy humor, had knocked him down. The clouds rolling across the tops of the old chestnut trees are black, and in the darkness that has followed the orchidaceous light my father is a blurred figure — somewhat past thirty years of age, with heavy dark hair that has already become gray enough to suggest to my mother's brothers that she is waiting to be married to an old man. They are uneasy because their only unmarried sister is nearly twenty-two and my father, during a long courtship, has failed to propose marriage. For me to know that this man survived the lightning's thrust is important, since, having survived, he married my mother. And my "memory" of that blurred figure — so remarkably alive in the presence of the two dead men, and at the same time helpless — may well be the only magic I have ever known. The fact remains that I, without knowing how or when it happened, have become, in a sense, that helpless figure.

I stayed in my comfortable chair until dinnertime. Afterward, when Jonathan was ready for bed, I went to his room in the hope of finding him restored to himself. Seeing me, however, he again lowered his head and said, "Go home."

Confidently then, I waited in the hall outside Jonathan's room while Eric turned off the light and closed the door. And there I remembered the way my father had smiled on that dull August morning when he said, "Belle, it's a terrible thing to be a grandmother."

Amused by the jocular tone of his voice, I had smiled, too. But now, being a grandmother who, like Mrs. Baker, seemed to have become a witch, I could not smile.

THE BURNING BUSH

NOTHING, I suspect, is too small to change the course of our lives. The starling caught in a jet engine, the shots fired at Sarajevo, that virus we took during the excitement of a wedding reception — all are little things that not only have changed the course of life but ended it. On the other hand, there are little things — the white violets that bloom in the swamp where our dogs hunt for the burrows of groundhog and muskrat, and the burning bushes, growing and "burning" in the most unexpected places — that, without really changing the course of our lives, help to direct them. At any rate, it was because of a burning bush growing where my grandfather's apple orchard died that George and I, having reached the time of life when love for the children we once were seems to outweigh all other love, were able to share a second childhood. This is a true wonder, all things considered.

Personally, I had hoped that after forty years of marriage our ways of seeing things might have become as similar as two halves of a clamshell. But George says, "No. We don't see things the same, because we weren't brought up the same way."

"I'm sorry."

"Oh, don't be sorry. You can't help the way you were brought up. Nobody can. I wish my mother could've raised you. She'd have made a wonderful woman out of you."

George's remarks on this subject have the solid sound that surmises after much repetition often have, and although I consider them an oversimplification of the truth, I learned long ago to throw an arc of smiling consent across a considerable difference of opinion. I smile now. "Why don't *you* make a wonderful woman out of me? It isn't too late."

"No. We don't see eye to eye. And we never will."

"I can't see that it makes much difference — after all we've been through together. Our *second* childhoods will be the same."

I still doubt that George's childhood was very different from my own. As a member of the Adams clan, he grew up in a busy company of well-fed children, while I, an only child, was born into a family of aging adults who, being neither idle nor hungry themselves, had failed to see how often I was both. But surely this was not difference enough to account for George's saying, out of what seemed to me to be conversationally a clear blue sky, "Belle, you're closer to the animals than anybody I know. The Minuits are more like *animals* than people." Yet, in his full baritone voice, it did sound like the truth.

I was less offended by this than might be supposed, for George is fond of animals and shares my concern for the survival of any toads, blacksnakes, and turtles that may have wandered into the path of the mowing machine. And when, as sometimes happens when we cut the fields, an animal is killed or a bird's nest destroyed, we beg each other's pardon and mourn, as if for a member of the family. I mourn, too, for the small trees and lovely flowers that are lost to the mower's whirling knives. But this is a grief that George does not share, because, he says, "Belle, that's not the way an Adams thinks. If you wanted to sell those trees, what would you get for them?"

I first saw the burning bush on a sunny afternoon in late October, when, having collected the ax, the handsaw, and the long-handled clippers, George and I went to the field on the upper side of the slope — where, according to my father, two apple orchards had starved to death — to cut bushes. "Wait, George," I said. "Here's a tree under this big sumac that we must save."

"Why? What is it?"

"It's something very special," I said, quite breathless because suddenly, instead of the sapling's bright leaves and brighter berries, I could see the child I used to be.

"It looks exactly like every other bush to me. What is it?"

"I don't know. It's a miracle."

Clearly then, I remembered the tall shrub — in the prime of its life when I was a child — that was like this bush. And now that I thought of it, I could feel the shrub's sinewy limbs, delightfully smooth, under the bare feet of the child I had been. In those faraway days, when I slipped to the ground the shrub leaned forward, its arms akimbo on the whitewashed fence, while I stood in the garden, spellbound, because, in the green sky of its shade, that big bush — it was really a small tree — held more constellations of four-pointed stars than I could count. The greatest wonder of all was that the stars of the bush, instead of being red, white, or blue, as stars ordinarily are, were purple. Now, looking back to my childhood, I wondered how it was that my father, who hated bushes even more perhaps than George does, and in the month of August, on a day that he fondly referred to as Plant Fatal Day, regularly began a war on them, had allowed one to lean on the garden fence. It was possible, certainly, for that remarkable bush to have had the gift of delitescence, but it seemed more likely, I thought, that my grandmother — who had persuaded my grandfather to buy the farm because, as a little girl, she had known this land and loved it, willfully and unreasonably, as I do — simply had told my father not to touch that bush. Otherwise, he surely would have cut it down.

"Well," George said, "it's growing where I want to see nothing but grass."

"*Please* keep it."

George dropped his ax. "What's the use of being out here?" he said. "I don't know what we're supposed to be doing. Do you?"

"Yes, we're cutting bushes," I said. "My father would turn over in the cemetery if he could see how close to the woods our fields have grown."

But George had started toward the house. I was talking to myself.

Later, one hot Saturday morning the following summer — time for me to be indoors, doing what my mother had called "redding up" — I remembered the handsome little bush on the upper side of the slope, and, instead of following the path that leads down the slope to the house, I waited for George to bring the mowing machine around to the side of the strawberry patch, where I had been pulling weeds. It was a great blessing, I thought, that George, who hates weeds as well as bushes, had bought a rotary mower and learned to use it. Thinking then of my own relationship with George, I noticed that the excitement of our very first meeting, when I was a freshman in college — an excitement so curiously compounded of fear and admiration that in the beginning I suffered a slight paralysis whenever we met — had not only survived forty years of marriage but was at this very moment making me a little short of breath. The next instant, he probably would stop the tractor and say, "What's the *matter?*"

George has a special way of saying, "What's the matter?" It is almost as though the sight of me — unexpectedly near — had frightened him. At any rate, seeing me often turns the four vertical lines between his eyebrows into exclamation points. Standing up to my elbows in daisy fleabane, I could see the two vertical wrinkles, flanked on both sides by a diagonal one, in the wide space between George's eyebrows.

George stopped the tractor and turned off the ignition and said, "What's the *matter?*"

"Nothing. I'm *happy.*"

"Go on, say what's on your mind."

No longer frowning, George seemed to be looking at something suspended about six inches above and behind my head. This habit of overlooking me when we met had been formed soon after George's employment as a public school teacher of mathematics, and was due, I imagined, to the fact that I had interrupted him in the process of solving a problem. "Are you listening?" I asked.

"Yes. Go on."

"But you're thinking about something else."

Sometimes when George fails to respond to my attempts to confide, I consider the possibility that he may be getting deaf. However, when I ask him whether or not he can hear me, his answer invariably is "I'm deaf in one ear, but the other one's all right. The trouble with you is that you don't talk plain." On this occasion, he simply said, "Talk plain, Belle."

I laughed, because in the beginning of our marriage there had been entirely too much of this; it seemed to me now that the need for "plain talk" had passed. As a matter of fact, I would have talked even more fancifully than Coleridge did in "Kubla Khan," if that were possible. "All right," I said. "I was thinking about the bush that used to be down there — near the fir." My left hand, with its palm held open and upward, was extended in the general direction of the house. And since George rarely quibbled over minor deviations from the truth, I decided not to amend this remark, even though I knew that the bush I was thinking of could never have been anywhere but under the big sumac, where I had found it in October.

"What about it?"

"We must *keep* it."

"Why, for heaven's sake? I'm tired of bushes. I want to get out of the sticks and set up a tent in the middle of Times Square."

"I know you do. But that has nothing to do with keeping this one little bush. Come and look at it. It's blooming now."

Earlier visits to see the little bush had been disappointing. This is not to say that George had refused to peer with me into the shade of the sumac; only that while peering his thoughts had seemed to be elsewhere. And now, having eased himself from the tractor and walked with me to the north side of the sunny field where, so long ago, my grandfather's apple orchard had been, George's silence indicated, almost certainly, that the slender sapling with its dark green leaves and fairy flowers was no more impressive in summer than it had been on that day in late fall when its seedpods hung, like bright pink popcorn from short strands of invisible wire.

"Well, what is it?" George asked.

"I was just thinking that we never mentioned the tree

like this that used to grow near the house. None of us did. I wonder how it happened to be the one unmentionable thing there was — aside from love."

Later, when George mounted the tractor and started it, I noticed that, in the event the tractor moved into the hedgerow while he was thinking of something else, the stump of an old apple tree was there to shield the sapling from the mowing machine. And when the mower passed me, with its whirling blades in full swing, I shouted, "There's a big stump in that clump of sumacs. Watch out for it."

"Thank you, I will," George said.

Pleased by the visit with George and the odd little tree, I started to go down the narrow path that zigzags from the strawberry patch to the house with those memories of my mother that the prospect of housecleaning on a Saturday afternoon always brought to mind. There had been good reasons, presumably, for her way of redding up — doing it all at once at the end of the week, as if she had just returned from a six-day trip and found the house waiting, alone, in the shadow of the woods. Until her death, I envied the deftness with which, after a week of working in the fields, she had baked the Saturday sponge cake and coconut custards while she polished the kitchen stove and scrubbed the sandstones that lay like two wide welcoming mats at each end of the kitchen. I remember with great pride her ability to move an avalanche of housework on a Saturday afternoon. But, without her deftness, my mother's way of dealing with a week's housework in a single afternoon had left so much of it undone that, thinking it could wait a little longer, I went to find my father's copy of Gray's

School and Field Book of Botany in the attic. There, listening to the humming of the wasps and breathing the musty
fragrance of cedar shingles baking in the sun, I wondered
what shocking ambivalence of mind had made it possible
for my father to have held this old schoolbook gently — as
though its binding had been made of live human skin —
and at the same time kill the bird that was singing momentarily in my heart by saying, *"Don't* stand so *close,* Belle."
Oddly enough, years later, George had used the same tone
of voice to say, "Belle, you're nothing but a clinging vine."
Greatly offended by this, I had complained to my mother,
who, stirring into the pot of boiling beef and cabbage that
was on the stove, said, "George is a smart man. You
might've done much worse."

When George came to the house an hour later, the redding up was still undone. "Did you learn anything?" he
said.

His habit — the natural result, I thought, of thirty years
as a teacher — of asking me this question whenever he
came into the kitchen after a few hours' absence had a
tendency to alienate my affections. This time, however, I
welcomed it. For one thing, George looked directly at me
so that I could see the fool's gold in his eyes, and, for another, I *had* learned something. "I know the name of the
bush that is growing under the big sumac."

"What is it?"

"Let me read what the book said about it."

"No, just tell me in your own words."

Hoping to see George smile, I said, "I'm going to read
the book's description. It's *funny.*"

"Is it a long-winded article?"

"No, you know how Gray's *Botany* is written."

"All right. I'm listening." Wherewith George dropped into the huge wing chair that was a part of his inheritance from his mother, and closed his eyes.

"The book says, 'A shrub not twining — in contrast to *Celastrus scandens*.' Or me," I added.

"Go on. For goodness' sake."

"All right. 'A shrub not twining — in contrast to *Celastrus scandens*, the common bittersweet. Wild from New York — west and south — and commonly planted.' "

"But what's its name?"

"*Celastrus euonymous atropurpureus.*"

"Talk plain. In English."

"The burning bush." Whereupon my mind made one of those circular movements that are the result of my inclination to see life as a series of overlapping circles — both translucent and rainbow-tinted, like the scales of an unthinkable fish — and I said, "I'm happy as Thoreau might've been if he had found the hound he lost."

Opening his eyes and blinking as though suddenly the sun had begun to shine in his face, George said, "What do you mean?"

"Hasn't everybody lost a hound?"

"No. All I ever had was a little black dog."

"And you lost him?"

"He went swimming with us in the Delaware River and drowned in the Lalor Street lock."

"I'm so sorry."

"That's what I hate about having pets."

"I had a black and white puppy when I was six years old,

and one morning while I was getting ready to go to school she followed the team that hauled charcoal to the hill. The team came back without her, and I watched the fields, calling her, for almost a week before my mother told me that a telephone pole had rolled off the wagon and broken her back. Why didn't someone tell me she was dead?"

"People don't think, Belle. People are cruel as hell."

"Speaking of cruelty, we must cut down those sumacs on the side of the field where we found the burning bush. It will need the sun."

"What's wrong with doing it now?"

"Oh, I can't. The house looks even more neglected than it did when I was a child."

"You don't have to go with me to cut bushes."

"But I want to go with you."

"All right, let's go."

"June isn't the time of year to cut bushes. Why can't we do it in August?"

"On Plant Fatal Day."

"Yes."

"When is Plant Fatal Day?"

"I don't know."

"That's what I thought."

"Wait, and we'll ask our Amish neighbors. They'll know."

"No. I must do things when they're on my mind. If I don't, I forget them. Get the ax."

"Wouldn't you like some coffee?"

"Yes. But don't you bother. I'll get it myself."

"Aren't you hungry? It's nearly noon."

"No. Are you?"

"Yes. Let's have an early lunch."

"You can't be hungry. I feel like we just had breakfast."

So I left the house and went to the wooden building where we now store tools and where my mother, fifty years ago, kept the flock of Leghorn hens to which — as one of her many experiments in crossbreeding — she had introduced a purebred gamecock. In fact, in the beginning, there had been *five* fighting cocks, and, true to their breeding, they fought. Shocked by the sight of so many heads all bloody and unbowed, she had with characteristic dispatch brought an ax from the woodshed and taken four of the gamecocks to the kitchen — headless. My memory of this incident prompted me to say, when George met me on the back porch, "I'll use the ax. You take the shears."

"Don't forget to drink your coffee, Belle. I've had mine."

"Wait for me," I said. "Wait for me." But George was moving in a straight line toward the sumac and did not turn his head.

Since, almost certainly, he was not going to wait, I went into the kitchen, where, momentarily, the presence of my mother seemed more real than my own. And there, making a cup of instant coffee and going, cup and saucer in hand, to sit in George's place at my grandmother's cherry table, instead of myself I was the child I used to be. It was to find this child who had somehow been left behind when we moved away from the farm that George and I had come back to this house, and finally, I thought, the child was found. Alone with my mother, as I had been after my father's death and during all of his absences, I asked her now, "Do you feel lonely?"

Assuming that her answer would be "Yes," I was pleased to hear her say "No."

"That's good. I was afraid you might be."

"No. I couldn't do anything with him."

She had been thinking, I guessed, of those awful hours when, suddenly frantic in the face of death, my father had tried to escape from their room and "go home," where, presumably, he might be "born again."

It was a good thing to have seen such wonders in a lifetime, I thought when I started to follow the zigzag path to the top of the slope, where George obviously was doing something he had wanted to do for a long time. The day was an unusually warm one, and I said, "Take it easy. We don't have to cut all of the bushes today, you know."

A few minutes later, I stooped to lift the burning bush from the ground, its green leaves and purple flowers already wilted.

"What's wrong?" George asked. "What's the *matter?*"

George rarely laughs. Instead, he smiles, letting his smile drain downward until the entire length of him is filled with amusement. At such times, a barely perceptible vibration shakes his body. I burst into sobs. Through my tears, I could see that he was *shaken*. "You promised to let it grow." As soon as I spoke, I remembered that George had made no such promise. Whenever we looked into the shade of the sumac, he had stood by without saying a word.

"You know how absentminded I am. You must forgive me," he said.

Had he stopped laughing, I might have forgiven him, but he continued to stand quietly erect and vibrant with laughter while both the little bush and the child I used to be died on the ground where we stood.

Wordless, I dropped the ax and ran toward the house where I was born and where George, because his childhood was happier than mine, cannot follow.

This is not quite the end of the story. In the backyard at our grandchildren's home, a burning bush grows — so large it is really a tree. It is taller than the one that shaded my grandmother's garden, and its branches have a certain uniformity — perhaps in response to our grandchildren's need for a place to play. Lacking my grandmother's garden fence to lean on, this tree has a stout, straight trunk, with its bark planed to a fine patina by the sneakered feet of its climbers.

Visiting there while Eric and Joan take a vacation, George and I stand in Joan's many-windowed kitchen, spellbound, while Isabel, Hans, and Jonathan hang, like sloths, from the lower branches of this tree, until a sudden access of pure delight and the pressure of their toes on the trunk carry them skyward. We watch, too, while Susan, who is five and too short of limb to scale the tree's smooth trunk unaided, carries a small stepladder from the house and settles it under the tree, to find that even then she is too short to reach the lowest branch. Up to this time, she had accepted our presence with a taut deference that in a less loved and loving child might have turned to tears or noisy expressions of dislike. We watch her, wondering whether she will cry. But Susan, exulting, comes running.

"Mom-mom," she says, "will you come and help me into the tree?"

Miraculously then, as Susan's weight is lifted from my arms, I feel the bark of my grandmother's burning bush — delightfully smooth — under the bare feet of the child I once was. And George, watching from a kitchen window, smiles — absentmindedly.

xiii

DROPOUTS IN SEPTEMBER

I SUSPECT that nothing short of heart failure would have induced George to stop teaching in the suburban school where for nearly thirty years he taught arithmetic and tried to share his faith in our public school system with doubtful pupils. Nor was that faith ever shaken by his failure to have shared it — as mine so soon was when I ventured into the schoolroom to teach — because George, unlike myself and other dropouts he has known, did not seem to have expected learning to be easier than it is. Perhaps, like Emerson, he has known all along that a man, when given the choice between truth and repose, must *choose.* Certainly it is as though, in George's mind, living and learning and teaching have become one and indivisible. And while he, speaking of a recent school dropout, warms to his subject I listen because the truth of the matter is that George — long ago and unbelievably — dropped out of high school.

Listening, I remember my enrollment in a normal school and say, "I didn't graduate from high school either, George."

"But you should have. You'd be a better person. If you had."

I doubt this and wonder why George still thinks of his failure "to get a high school diploma" with a sense of shame. Beside my own failure to have become a teacher it seems to me a small failure. "All right. Tell me about *this* dropout."

"I told him to stay and get that diploma."

"Didn't he listen to you?"

"He listened. But the sound of my voice never reached his brain. I said to him, 'Your ears hear me but your mind is gone. I was the same kind of mule — at your age. Go ahead. Quit school.'"

"What did he say?"

"He said, 'It's too embarrassing to come to school while my father's in jail.'"

"That *would* be embarrassing, George."

"I told him it would be more embarrassing if he didn't stay in school."

"What is his name?"

"Melvin Boone. Aged sixteen."

"Bright?"

"Yes. Very bright."

At this point the fact that Melvin Boone had left school, rejecting the truth for those difficulties that the truth-seeker habitually associates with repose, was dropped from our conversations. Melvin's unexpected appearance in our yard two years later, however, recalled that fact along with many others.

It was one of those warm days, just before the frosts come, when the Michaelmas daisies begin to bloom and men who have outlived their ambitions die. At any rate, on such a day my grandfather had died and — thirty-nine years later — his only son, my father. To be exact it was on this very date, twelve years earlier, that my father died. In a way, therefore, it was natural for Melvin Boone's visit to seem more like a *visitation* — his presence a little more like the "angel" my father had meant when he, noticing the approach of a hobo, said, "We may be entertaining an angel unaware" — than the unannounced arrival of one of George's former pupils usually does.

"Summer's almost gone, George." Looking from one of the living room windows, I saw a long black station wagon going north and raising a tower of red dust on the new road, and since traffic in the direction of our neighbor's peach orchard often is brisk at this time of year, I thought that the young man in the station wagon was going to buy a basket of peaches for his mother (or a grandmother) who just now had remembered how short a time the peach harvest is.

"I know," George answered from his place at the kitchen table where he was drinking a cup of coffee. "I can feel winter coming."

"Winter is a long way off. You miss being back in school."

"No, I don't. I hated school."

"So did I. But now I miss the long walk through the woods and the smell of falling leaves and the little inkwells. Did your desk have a little inkwell?"

"Yes. Everybody's did."

"I had a little blue pail with an apple and two thick slices of apple-butter bread in it."

"Apple-butter bread? That's good."

"Not when everybody else has chocolate cake and fried chicken. But all that's changed. I can buy as much chicken as I want and you're a retired teacher without a worry in the world. You don't feel the winter coming. And neither do I."

"You will when you're as old as I am."

George is four years older than I am. But the difference in our feelings on this September day, I suspect, has little to do with the number of years we have lived. "You want to be in school."

"I don't. I wasn't a teacher."

"Eric says that you were one of the best teachers he ever had."

And beyond the window, where a spindrift of red dust was settling into a field of butterfly weeds and wild carrot, I could see George standing before the blackboard of his classroom — a thresher with both hands on the handle of his flail — while grains of truth, in a flurry of chaff, fell from the heavy-headed pupils before him.

"Eric is my son. He has to believe that I was a teacher."

"And you've never stopped being one."

"No, I'm an old man. I've nothing to give to others now."

Then the dogs barked and, looking out, I saw that the long black station wagon was parked behind George's car in the yard. "That boy must be lost," I said. "I'll go out."

Certainly, on the basis of our experience with the others who had lost their way to the peach orchard, it was probable that the driver of the station wagon would wait where he was for directions.

When I rounded the corner of the house, however, he was jogging toward me in the shade of an old blue spruce that is so tall and slender that at noon when our young evergreens have squat shadows (or none at all) its shadow reaches across the lawn, like an arm extended in greeting, and visitors quite often stop to ask, "What is it? I never saw a tree like it. It must have a wonderful root system."

But this visitor hurried forward without giving the old tree a glance. "Is Mr. Adams at home?" he said.

This is one of those diffident former pupils, I thought, who will give me his name and, while I announce it to George, sit on a terrace bench that overlooks the meadow until my husband either joins him there or invites him to come indoors. And since the majority of George's former pupils did this, I was truly surprised when this boy moved abreast of me in the direct line he almost certainly would have taken if I had not been present. This was the way Eric — with his career and marriage in mind — had crossed the lawn with me in the spring before my father died. Then we had approached the old spruce from its western side. "You're wrong, Mother," Eric was saying. "I'm not running *away*. I'm running *to* something." So I stood in the shade of the old spruce tree — the roots of which seemed to be my roots — and waved while he drove away. It seemed incredible that, on the day of its planting, I had expressed my joy by jumping over this tree until my mother, fearing an injury to the little spruce or myself, begged me to stop. And cheerfully I ran away.

Now this boy, like Eric, was running *to something* and, at the same time, he was saving his breath.

Moreover the way he was dressed — new sun tans, shining loafers, and a pullover that was snug at the neck to a degree that Eric's seldom was — suggested that he was not one, as I in faded blue jeans and one of George's old shirts so obviously was, to underestimate the need for neatness. Surely, I thought, there was nothing in his appearance that might have caused his mother to say, "What are you running away from, my son?" Yet the alacrity with which he followed me into the kitchen was even more remarkable than the silent march that preceded it.

But George, seeing us come pell-mell through the pair of doors that we and our four-footed friends ordinarily use with caution, got up from the table and, holding out his hand, said, "Hello, hello. How are you, Melvin?"

"You certainly have a good memory, Mr. Adams."

George modestly protested the boy's compliment and, after shaking hands with him, said, "Belle, this is Melvin Boone."

As I remember it, neither Melvin nor I acknowledged this introduction. It was not necessary, really, because George immediately led the way to our living room and, indicating a small cane-backed sofa, said, "Sit here. I'm sorry now I scared Belle into buying this size. We should've spent a little more money and bought a full-length piece of furniture. I'm a coward when it comes to buying furniture."

"It's very nice," Melvin said, sitting down beside George. "I want to talk to you, Mr. Adams."

"Go ahead. Say what's on your mind."

"I worked with my father this summer. But I've another job now."

"Then you can go to night school and get your diploma."

"Yes, I want to register right away."

"*Get that diploma.* Don't let anything stop you."

"Oh, I won't."

I seldom hear the word "cozy" apart from "tea" without suspecting the person who used it of either condescension or a willingness — after assuming that I am condescending — to use this word instead of another four-letter word to bolster his or her courage. Yet, oddly enough, I could not think of a better way to describe the appearance of Melvin Boone and my husband on our new "distressed wood" sofa.

"Go ahead, Melvin. Say what's on your mind."

"Oh, I will. That's why I want to talk to you."

"All right. Go ahead. Don't ever be afraid to say the truth."

"Do you remember my father?"

"He's one of the best salesmen I ever knew. How is he?"

"Well. I've been working with him this summer."

"You can learn an awful lot from him."

"But I don't want to get in *trouble*."

"Is he living with you?"

"No."

"Are you living with your mother?"

"Yes."

"You're going to stay with her, aren't you?"

"I'm going to stay with my mother."

"That's right. She's a good woman. You stick to her."

"I will. I will."

"How old are you?"

"Eighteen."

"Are you working now?"

"I have a job and I'm going to work next week."

"Then you can go to school and get your high school diploma?"

"Yes, I want to get my diploma."

Melvin's ability to express the truth, as George saw it, was so much greater than my own — my long familiarity with my husband's viewpoint notwithstanding — that I smiled to myself, thinking that whatever the boy's former difficulties were the end of them was in sight. Certainly there had been no need for George to say (as in our many years together I had heard him say), "We don't see eye to eye. We weren't *raised* the same way. Your parents meant well but didn't seem to know the first thing about *handling* you."

Now, after a short pause in which both occupants of the love seat seemed to be gathering strength for a shift in their mental gears, George said, "What are you going to do — next week?"

"Sell."

"You must've learned a lot from your father this summer. About selling."

"My father can sell *anything*."

"I know he can. I envy that gift above all others, I guess."

"I'm a pretty good salesman myself," Melvin said.

Having cleared the table of our luncheon dishes and bread crumbs, I said, "I'll bet you are. You remind me of Eric. A little."

"Why not? I'm sold on heredity." Drumming on the wooden arm of the sofa very fast with the fingers of his left hand, George repeated, "But get that high school diploma."

"I will."

"Don't put it off. I had you in the tenth grade and I know you have a good mind. *Use it.*" George's smile, while continuing to be sympathetic, had turned a shade stoical.

At the same time Melvin, his pale face suddenly appearing less young and innocent, seemed ready to do just that. "So I wanted to talk to you. I have a job now and my mother thought that if you paid the rent for a month we could stay in our apartment."

"How much is that?"

"A hundred dollars."

"Is it a nice apartment? Or do you want to move?" George asked.

"Oh no, we'd like to stay. It's a nice, clean place. But we're back three months in our rent and the landlord is getting mean about it."

"Why?" I said. "When he knows you have a job and will pay him?" It was unthinkable that the landlord had never learned of the blessings that come to those who are kind to other people — and "angels" in disguise. "You remember Lot's experience, Belle." The words, echoing across the years since his death, had lost none of the resonance of my father's booming voice. "Be kind to strangers. We never know when, like Lot, we may be entertaining angels."

"He must be paid today. He didn't say why."

"How much does he want?" George said, thinking, I imagine, of a fraction of one hundred.

"One month's rent. Or three, if you want to pay all of it." Melvin's voice was quick and gay as the voice of a hostess might be when, passing a plate of tiny sandwiches at a tea party, she says, "One? They are so *small*. Take three."

"What do you think, Belle? Shall we give this young man a check?"

"Of course," I said, thinking that the only thing to be decided now was "How much?"

At this point my father's presence was so real that I could see him taking his worn billfold from a threadbare hip pocket and holding it within easy reach of my outstretched hand. He had not asked if a gift should be given, only "How much do you want, Belle?" And although death had silenced that question forever, it seemed now that I smelled the mustiness of cigar smoke and much-handled money that scented his purse while he lived.

"Where is the checkbook?" George said.

I took the checkbook from my desk and George, having written a check for one hundred dollars, prepared a receipt for that amount and asked Melvin to sign it. And he did, letting his name slant upward from the scrap of paper with cheerful exuberance. A moment later George returned the checkbook, with Melvin's IOU, to the desk drawer. Whenever I open that drawer, I can see Melvin's signature there with its final letters — "n" and "e" — carefully made a little larger than the rest of his name. It is as if, believing that persons who are careless with the final letter in a word will be suspected of dishonesty, Melvin deliberately enlarged his "finals." "Shall we send the money to your landlord?" I asked him.

"Oh no, he wants to be paid today. I'll pay him right away." Flushed and smiling, Melvin looked directly at me for the first time. "I'll start paying you back next week — five dollars at a time. I'll send it. Or, I'll bring it. Then I could visit with you." He had underscored the last pronoun lightly — but surely.

When the door had closed behind Melvin, George said, "That boy made me nervous. I must go away."

"Goodbye. But hurry back. He made me nervous, too."

"Do you think we should've given him a check?"

"Yes."

"But don't we need it?"

"Not as much as he did."

"I should've talked to his mother first. Forgive me."

"Forgive you? You did the only thing you could've done."

"Let me go away for a while. I'm upset."

"All right. But hurry back."

*

It was Melvin, however, who hurried back and, panting as if he had run a long way, asked to see George. The black station wagon was parked where George's car had been and once again Melvin and I met in the shadow of the old spruce. "Mr. Adams is not here," I said.

"Where is he?

"On the road."

"On the road?"

Then seeing that Melvin's disappointment was too keen to be taken lightly, I said, "It's a kind of game that Mr. Adams plays since his retirement from teaching. I don't know exactly what he does when he gets to the road." But when I smiled to show that this was an everyday occurrence that both of us enjoyed, Melvin did not smile. "He'll be here soon. Why don't you wait in your car?"

"Why don't I talk to you until he comes?" And again the boy displayed his remarkable ability to enter a house without that awkward gyration the opening of two doors imposes on me. "Or are you awfully busy?"

"I am busy."

"Then I'll sit and gaze."

I edged the chair he seemed to have chosen into a more receptive position under an oil painting Eric had exhibited locally and named "Somber Thoughts." "How's that?"

"Fine, thank you." Gazing at the painting then without sitting down, he said, "How is Eric doing?"

"Very well."

"What does he do to earn a living?"

"He writes. Didn't you know?"

"Yes. I guess I did hear something about Eric's success." Seated now, the boy's resemblance to our son had dis-

appeared entirely and I saw him as an intruder with tense
shoulders and a sallow face in which the dark eyes — unlike
those clear transparencies through which Eric, at eighteen,
had looked and seen so much — were opaque and immov-
able as the eyes of a statue, although presumably not sight-
less.

"It's a business." I smiled at Melvin, hoping to see that
on account of Eric's "business" and the precious time I
had taken from my own business to speak of it, he was smiling, too. But he, presumably, was "gazing" at something
else.

"My mother said, when I talked to her just now, that if
Mr. Adams could give me another check she would help
to repay it." Then, looking quickly at my grandmother's
clock on the shelf, he asked, "Is that time right?"

"Yes, I think so."

"When will Mr. Adams come back?"

"In less than an hour."

"Does the bank close at three?"

"Yes. But you still have time to get there. It's two-
thirty."

"Could you give me a check?"

"For two hundred dollars?"

"Yes."

"No, Mr. Adams likes to be consulted before I write a
check of that size. And he'll be here any minute. While
we're waiting, why don't you tell me about your father.
What's he like?"

The boy's likeness to our son had been left in the shade
of the spruce tree this time. He was a complete stranger
who, during George's absence, had to be faced alone. But I

know September. I know it as one of the turning points of
the year — a time when, if ever, a visit could turn out to
have been a visitation. And so, while Melvin's second appearance was more vexing than his first one had been, it
seemed to have deeper implications.

The vibrations of my father's voice, too, were quite
audible. "Give him something to eat and let him sleep in
the barn, Cotty. We may be entertaining an angel." None
of those strangers who, from time to time, wandered from
the dusty road to our back door ever turned out to have
been angels. Nor were we left any the worse for having
given them a night's shelter in the barn with bread and
coffee in the morning. So, my mother, wide-eyed and afraid
because some of these had looked *very* strange and talked
to themselves in a foreign language, invariably obeyed.
"We must not get the penny too close to the eye, Cotty.
(That was the pet name my father had given my mother
long before I was born.) The Lord loves a cheerful giver,
you know."

Now Melvin was saying, "We had everything when my
father lived with us."

"You did?"

"Yes, we had everything. He gave us *everything*."

"Why do you think he did that?" I knew the question
was unfair. I had no more right to question the generosity
of Melvin's father than I had to doubt my father when
he said, "We may be entertaining an angel."

And Melvin, looking down at the bare pine floor on
which his polished loafers rested, blushed. "I don't know.
He was that way."

Unfairly too, I remembered the way Eric had said,

"Mother, I had everything I really needed." He had not said that he lacked nothing. In fact Melvin alone — of all the persons I know — *had everything*. And, unable to doubt that it was true, I repeated my question. "But why? Men aren't generous by nature."

"Mr. Adams is."

"Mr. Adams tries to be helpful. Some people are generous without trying to be helpful. There's a difference."

"I know how Mr. Adams is. When I had him in school, he talked to some of the boys by the hour."

"In that case, why wasn't he asked to resign, do you think?"

"Oh, I don't mean that he spent *too* much time with any one boy."

"That's good to know." Laughing, I looked at the clock and wondered how much time George was going to spend with whoever it was that he was talking to now. "He does try to be helpful."

"Nobody knows that better than I do," Melvin said soberly. "I wish more schoolteachers were like him."

"I'll tell him you said that. He found teaching a discouraging job."

"He's still teaching, isn't he?"

"Only as a substitute teacher. But there's plenty to do here — on the farm."

"That's right. You used to live in town, didn't you? I remember the house. It's a nice place."

"Yes. We lived there a long time, with my parents, and when we sold it there were some who said that we stole that house from my parents. But that's not true. They gave us the money to buy this farm on condition that we keep them here until they died. If you've ever lived with old people, you know it's not easy to take their house, or anything else that is theirs, from them."

"No, it's not easy," Melvin said.

After which both Melvin and I retired, at my suggestion, to the yard to see a huge maple tree that, without warning, one July night had exploded. "We heard three reports that sounded like gunfire at close range and thought the revolution had begun. It was the most frightening thing I ever heard. And lightning often strikes quite close to this house on account of its elevation and the woods nearby. But this was a human sound. If the sounds made by a firing squad can be called human." Pointing to the roots of a Virginia creeper that clung to the broken heart of the tree, I said, "It's incredible that one seed could've carried so much force, isn't it?"

At this observation Eric might have encouraged me to make any number of nonsensical deductions. But Melvin, looking a shade more sallow, said, "How long will Mr. Adams be gone?"

"Not much longer."

The next moment, indeed, we saw George's car stop to pick up the day's mail and Melvin followed me into the kitchen for the third and last time. There he repeated to George what, an hour earlier, he had told me. "I talked to my mother and she says that if you will pay our rent for three months, she'll help me to pay you back."

"That's two hundred dollars *more*," George said, getting another complexion altogether.

"Yes. Three hundred with the money you gave me," Melvin said.

"No," George said, turning his back to me and looking, instead, at the ceiling. "I don't have that much."

"My mother said she would help me to repay you."

"I'll go with her to the office of public assistance," George said.

"Oh no," the boy said. "She couldn't do that."

"Why not?" George said. "If I needed money that's where I'd go. *I've been there.*"

George's determination to be helpful was, it seemed to me, taking him somewhat beyond the truth; for, as I remembered our time of need, it was to my father (interceding for both George and myself) that I went. And it had not been necessary to go further.

"We can't go there," Melvin said.

"I'd rather go there than to jail. Wouldn't *you?*"

Although visibly shaken by this change in George's manner, the boy's voice was firm. "We can't go there."

"Let me talk to your mother. She'll understand."

Melvin's pallor left him then and his skin brightened as if the realization that George was unwilling to give him *everything* had at last dawned on him. "I'll let you know when it will be convenient for my mother to see you, Mr. Adams," he said.

The hint of hauteur in his speech was worthy of an angel. And since Melvin has neither redeemed the IOU in my desk drawer nor returned to visit us, I like to think that his appearance was perhaps a *visitation* — suitable for dropouts in September.

xiv

A PICTURE OF YESTERDAY

AT DUSK on the evening before, Harvey (the younger of the Gruber brothers) had taken a flashlight from his hip pocket and preceded me to the cellar kitchen where his mother's dishes were piled along with other mementos too precious to be exposed to the night air.

"Look, Belle," he said, flashing light into the dark. "Do you know what it is?" He took the little bell from a dark shelf and swung it briskly from his cupped hand. "My father used to tie it to the tongue of his bobsled."

"I remember the bobsled. He took us for a sleigh ride in it — before you were born."

"People are crazy about old bells — now."

"My mother was. She loved bells."

"I've seen one of these small bells sold for fifty dollars," Harvey said.

"It's very nice. Really. Thanks for showing it to me."

It was not our intention to go to the Gruber sale, however, because neither George nor I wanted to see the mules sold. When our farm was sold, my parents had moved away without having a sale because the pain of seeing their livestock led from the barn, to be prodded and bid upon by the jocular crowd that collects around an auctioneer at a sale, was more than either one of them could bear. And so, when the piano had been hoisted into the broad bed of the hay wagon (where our three wooden beds, with their ropes neatly looped and draped from a bedpost, five tables of various sizes and degrees of antiquity, and nineteen plank-bottomed chairs — not forgetting my mother's green velour parlor suite — already were), my parents *moved*. To my undying regret, an ancient spinning wheel, the spool bed where I slept as a child (and waking, saw the fanciful creatures related, my mother said, to the fact that I had eaten too much meat for supper), and the worm-eaten drop leaf from which all of our meals were taken, had been left behind. "What in the world would we do with them in *town?*" my mother said. And her dark eyes flashed so that I was afraid to say that she might have stored them in the attic.

My father, with the exception of a two and one-half dollar

gold piece that disappeared in the excitement of our moving, had closed his eyes to my losses then as, almost twenty-five years later, I had been able to close my eyes to his sorrow when, once again, the piano, our four beds (the fourth one new and custom-made for Eric), six tables, and nineteen straight-backed chairs were moved. (My mother's parlor suite had been replaced by three cane-backed pieces and sold.)

This time, we had no domestic animals to leave in the care of our successors, our blind black cat having been killed by a stray dog shortly before the moving. And remembering how short the lives of our farm animals had been after our desertion of them, we accepted the cat's death as a part of the price one pays for moving. In fact my mother's horse and the older of my father's mules had died almost immediately and left Mike alone to be sold when the farm changed hands eight years later.

So that when George and I went to the Gruber sale on the day after Harvey showed the bell to me and Harvey led his mules from their stable and a jocular crowd gathered around them, my tears were for the heavy dark-skinned saddle mule my father had called Mike.

Interestingly, my mother (who loved bells and feared none of the animals) was very suspicious of that mule. "Don't go into the barnyard, Belle. Mike doesn't like small animals. He might strike you. And kill you."

To be kicked by a horse, mule, or cow was common enough. My mother, who was fonder of horses than people, had, when a little girl, been kicked senseless by a horse and still could feel, whenever she thought of it, the impact of an iron horseshoe on her midriff. The moral for me, therefore, seemed to be that all large domestic animals were quite capable of kicking little girls who unexpectedly wandered behind them. In short, I took a certain amount of kicking for granted. The thought of being *struck* by a mule, however, was strange enough to be a source of wonder.

And so, round-eyed, I often walked closer to Mike than otherwise I might have. Noting his quiet submission to the teamster's saddle that, when hauling charcoal or telephone poles to market, was superimposed on his harness and the pensive angle of his big head as he leaned forward in his traces, I saw no inclination to strike. Nor, indeed, had my father ever warned me of this possibility. "He was a fine saddle mule. There was none better in a cultivator either. I think that — next to Jack — he was the best mule I ever had."

Jack was light brown and long-legged. His age was unknown and his spirit so free from guile that, from the age of four, I rode him. He died on the farm where almost all of his life had been spent and when we returned from our adventure in suburban living, his ghost was at rest. It was Mike that we missed when, passing the open stable door, we remembered the six mules that once had filled the barn with their strength and raucous laughter. But it was only for Mike that we wished. With Mike at hand, my prolonged tuggings on the recalcitrant cord attached to the motor of our garden tractor would have been unnecessary. And my father, watching my struggle from a distance, might never have thought of saying, "Mike would've harrowed the garden by this time, Belle. There's nothing like a mule for gardening."

"That's right," I said, remembering those summer vacations from school when — no longer a little girl but suddenly a big one — I cultivated the tobacco with Mike. "He was very good with a harrow."

These short paeans in memory of Mike, naturally, had ended when my father died. And, just as naturally, I had forgotten them — until the day of Grubers' sale.

When Harvey Gruber led his mules into the clearing around the auctioneer, one of them raised his long head and, seeing us standing like mourners gathered about an open grave, seemed to be on the verge of *striking*. His eyes rolled backward as though a mulish intuition had warned him of the fact that his career was about to take one of those hairpin turns that, from time to time, forced mules and men to look backward. Harvey's hand on the mule's halter, however, was firm and the mules waited quietly for the bidding to begin. The crowd was quiet, too.

"What do I hear?" the auctioneer said. "One hundred dollars — for two good mules? You can buy one, or both. Will you start the bidding?" There was a ruffle of laughter, but no bid for either the single-line leader that all through the previous summer had walked, with a gently swinging stride, along the rows of peppers, corn, and squash — or the pair. "You know who'll buy these good mules, if you don't?" the auctioneer said.

My eyes searched the faces of the crowd and found one —coarse with the cruelty that destroyed the dodo — smirking. Mike's ghost moved then between us. It rolled on the bare ground and, covered with dust, got up to prance on its hind legs — like a playful kitten.

It might be possible, I thought, for George to buy

Harvey's mules and lead them across the meadow to live
the remainder of their days with Mike's ghost and the three
black cats that were living alone in our barn. "It would be
company for them," I told myself. But the barnyard wall
is in ruins and I have forgotten the witty exchange of sign
language and words that makes the society of mules a delight. George, unfortunately, never has lived with mules
and learned their ways.

So it happened that the mules were sold to the man
who had laughed alone while the auctioneer solicited his
bid and we bought the bell. More exactly, Mrs. Geiger —
friend since the years when we followed the winding road
to the little schoolhouse in the woods — bought it for us
because she had wanted us to be free to leave the sale
before the mules were sold.

Now, holding the loop of binder twine that, one moonlit
night in an otherwise forgotten winter, had held the little
brass bell to the tongue of Mr. Gruber's bobsled, I *ring* until
George says, "Stop it, Belle. You're a bad woman."

George takes a Janus-faced view of all relics and the
women who treasure them. It seems that he (having been
born in the second month of the twentieth century) has,
like Janus, an affinity for beginnings — not to mention gates
and doors — and, therefore, no time for the appreciation of
"old things." So I assume that when he calls me "a bad
woman" — as he often does — he does not mean that I lack
old-fashioned virtues but rather that I have had some of
them too long.

Resting now in the palm of my hand, the bell is squat and

serene. "Today is my mother's birthday," I say. "If she were alive, she would be ninety-three years old. I rang the bell for her."

"She was a good woman," George says. "I miss her." George often says that my mother was a good woman and that he misses her. And I nod, wondering how his habit of saying that she was "a good woman" and I a "bad woman" really began. Even more curious, perhaps, is my habit of agreeing with him.

"She would've loved this bell. She never had a bell like it."

My mother, indeed, had been so truly fond of the sound of sleigh bells that, after forgiving my father for spending the whole day at the Plow Hotel, she could not forgive him for buying there — instead of a high-backed cutter with chimes on its shafts — an old-fashioned swan's-nest sleigh without bells. Embarrassed both by my mother's tears and my father's habit of staying overlong at the local tavern, my grandfather reminded her that the old yellow sleigh, with its shallow body and wide-set runners, would be less likely to upset in snowdrifts than a cutter with chimes. But she was inconsolable although, to me, the old sleigh looked as merry as the pumpkin Cinderella's fairy godmother had turned into a golden coach. In reality, the yellow sleigh turned many a snowfall into a holiday on which my mother, slender and serene behind her sorrel trotter, came to school to the accompaniment of sleigh bells. Even when it was raining and she used her phaeton to take me home from school, the sight of her had suggested the sound of bells and singing on moonlit snow.

This bell that I hold now in my hand is encircled near its smallest circumference by a loose line of small flowers. Below them, on one side, is the date when, presumably, the bell was cast — 1878. The numerals are large enough to imply the historical importance of the year — the year of the Berlin Congress on the one hand and a union of German Socialists on the other to demand universal suffrage for Germans above the age of twenty, publication of *The Return of the Native* by Thomas Hardy in England and, in America, my mother's fifth birthday.

The date is embossed and flanked on each side by a slightly tipsy Greek cross. The name of a Swiss town (Saigonelier) fills the space below the two crosses. On the opposite side of the bell, arched like a pennant in the breeze, is the name "Chiantel." Two palmate arrangements of foliage and a straight-line rendition of the word "Fondeur" complete the decoration.

After we bought the bell at the sale, a woman of my age, the year and sign of the zodiac being the same, said, "Now you have a bell to put on George so you'll *know* where he is."

Interestingly enough, this woman's father — on the day after our memorable sleigh ride with the Grubers, in answer to a question of mine, "Did you hear us singing last night?" — had said, "Yes, we heard you and knew who it was. Only crazy people go sleighing in the moonlight. When there's no snow on the ground." The unexpected cruelty of these words rendered me dumb in his presence then and, for the rest of my life, cautious in the arms of pure joy. But my contemporary's remark, happily, had no long-lasting effects. I know now that bitter words do not entirely destroy one's happiness and say, "It's always nice to know where George *is*."

And it is good to hold the bell that Mr. Gruber once fastened to the tongue of his bobsled and remember that my parents, that moonlit night, sang, "After the Ball Is Over" and "Daisy, Daisy, I'm half crazy all for the love of you." Later, when the little bell rang from the tongue of Mr. Gruber's sled, I imagine that the snow was deep enough to allow smooth sledding and my parents considered themselves too old for singing the songs of the Gay Nineties.

While George studies the Sunday school lesson, I try to polish the bell but it is mottled with dark spots and, discouraged by their persistence, I complain. "It won't shine. What shall I do?"

"Have it polished. There are men who *polish* old metal."

"Like the dermatologist who took the keratoses from my face?"

"Perhaps."

"No, we won't have anyone polish it. The edelweiss might be burnished away."

"Do as you like. And don't ring."

After which the little bell starts to ring without the least effort on my part. "Don't you wish we had taken a picture of yesterday?"

"It was a beautiful day."

"I'll hang the bell from the arm of this reading lamp," I say. "Here I can see it — night and day."

Momentarily the edelweiss catches the sunlight and, in the dark space between Saigonelier and Chiantel Fondeur, I see a picture of *yesterday*.

XV

AND TOMORROW

"George?" I say and the little curved ears lean sharply in my direction. Then, with a soft whinny and a toss of his head, the big blue roan trots toward the barn where his blacksmith and I are waiting. His pasture is short and brown under a skin of snow; only the garlic is green among the dry stalks of last summer's Queen Anne's lace and he brings the odor of garlic with him.

At the same time, "George" brings the excitement that is both his excuse for being mine and (my husband says) my excuse for being. This had nothing to do with Emerson's well-known ode "The Rhodora." It means simply that I still dream of riding my own horse. That dream is as clear as it was when a lifetime ago I awoke to find that the Shetland pony I had so clearly seen was only a dream. The horse now in view is real but not, in reality, the horse of my dreams. And, although plainly proud of his appearance, he seems to feel my uneasiness.

"He has a nice little dogtrot." George stops where we are waiting and the blacksmith holds out the white nylon halter to him, so that he may feel it with his lips before accepting its hold on his head.

"It's funny to hear you say that. He runs in circles — just as the dogs do — when they see my husband. My husband calls him 'the big dog.'"

"Have you ridden much lately?"

"Not at all. Lately."

It is tactless, I think, to remind the blacksmith of my last time on George's back and how short a time it was because it was he who had said that George should be ridden before the ritual referred to as "shoeing." Instead of riding five miles, as the blacksmith suggested, I had — in less time than the telling takes — rolled from George's busy back into the barnyard dust bowl — where he, in more relaxed moments, rolls himself. Later, the blacksmith told me, "The saddle girth must be tight. No horse will put up with a loose *cinch*." To which I had replied, "The cinch was tight — until George let out all the air he had taken in while I tugged to make it tighter." But of course, since the blacksmith then saddled George and rode into his pasture and, dismounting said, "He's a good broke western horse and very comfortable to ride," I have been willing to believe that my unsettling experience was, indeed, not George's fault but mine. And, realizing how shocking —to George — my failure to ride him then was, I say nothing while the blacksmith leads him into his stable, ties him to the feed trough, and removes one of his shoes.

"Whoa, George. You're bigger than I am. All right, take it away. I know you're bigger than I am." The gentle muttering goes on until George, firm at last on three legs, takes a second lump of sugar from my hand and the black-smith, holding the fourth leg between his own two, has prepared the hoof for shoeing and shod it. Then, rolling his eyes, George yields up his left hind foot and the ritual proceeds.

"Good boy," I say. "I'll get you an ear of corn." And I do.

"The nails sting his feet when it's this cold."

"I didn't know that." What I do know, however, is that this big horse — cold, bored with the winter landscape, or suddenly aware of the fact that he is handsome enough to carry a king to his coronation — can do a spectacular hand-stand. I know, too, that in that event the blacksmith almost certainly would be rocketed into a haymow that is overhead.

To think of this possibility now makes my own feet tingle. But the blacksmith, in blissful ignorance (or is it grim de-termination?), says, "This would be a good day for fox hunting."

Since all I know of fox hunting is too depressing to be interesting to the blacksmith who believes, perhaps, as the

Greeks did, that hunting on horseback "keeps men from growing old," I agree with him that it is a good day for fox hunting. It does not matter — while George begs for another sugar cube — that the only fox hunter I ever knew was both old and blind when I knew him. Nor do the tears that I saw in his eyes on the day of the last hunt he ever attended move me the way they did then. Only the fox has survived — in sharp focus — to this day.

I see the fox lope across the snow to the hilltop where, two or three years earlier, my grandfather had come to meet me, after my first day of school. There the fox stops, looking over his shoulder at the hunting party for a minute before going on and out of sight. In my memory of that fox chase, I see no horses. Perhaps it is too soon for their riders to have taken them from the barn's shelter. I do see my grandfather standing in the empty circle that old age so often makes for us when we are in a crowd, staring with his poor eyes across the snow to the top of the hill where, just now, the fox was. And I see a sable foxhound leave the pack to lick my grandfather's hand.

My grandfather's sight was too close to blindness for him to be sure that this was the hound he recently had sold. But when we were at home that night, he said, "Driver came to me. He knew me." And I saw tears.

Afterward, when the man who had bought Driver called to say he had found him shot to death in his kennel, the tears were brushed away so quickly that I am not really sure they were there at all. "We have no idea who did it. Do you?"

"Yes," my grandfather said, looking very angry. "I do."
And I was deeply shocked to hear him name a man that
I had believed to be his dearest friend. It seems regrettable
— even now.

"Martin asked me the other day if I had seen Big George
lately," the blacksmith said.

"How is Martin? We haven't seen him in a long time."

"He's had a little trouble. But he's feeling better now."

Martin is the horse dealer who bought George at the
Grenoble auction and, after some misgivings, sold him to us.
Invariably polite, his eyebrows had twitched when, at our
first meeting, he said, "Wouldn't you like an older horse,
Mrs. Adams?" Later he told me, "I'm not sure that I want
to sell you that horse. He's been dancing on his hind feet.
Just a little." Finally, after considerable thought, he of-
fered to let me "try" George. "The boys admitted that
they were teasing him when he reared."

"It was Martin who named him 'George,' you know."

"It's a good name."

"It's my husband's name and means husbandman. I like
that."

"He was a very sick horse — when I saw him the first
time."

"Did you see him at Grenoble?"

"Yes."

"How did he behave — at the auction?"

"Good. Good."

"There's so much that I would like to know about
George. When I asked Martin what he knew he always

said, 'Only what we learned here on the farm. He seems to be well-mannered.' But it's not enough to know that he is a blue roan, eight years old, and seventeen hands high. Every horse has a history, doesn't he? I'd like to know where George was born and raised. And what he was trained to do. By whom? And why did they sell him? Yet Martin, if pressed for more information, always said, 'Perhaps you wanted an older horse, Mrs. Adams?' Once he said, 'How old are you?' And when I told him, he said, 'You must be a spunky one.' Martin didn't really want to sell me George, I guess."

"He's a nice horse," the blacksmith says. "Short back and high withers. Smart color. Is he for sale?"

"No. I'll keep him."

Then, driving the last nail into George's right rear hoof, the blacksmith said, "He's not a bad horse to shoe. Shall I write his name in my book?"

"Oh yes." Suddenly warm with the pride of a difficult undertaking well done, I take the last sugar cube from my pocket and give it to the horse. A moment later the blacksmith unbuckles the white halter that is part of the shoeing ceremony and George trots back to his pasture. It is a deferential performance cut short to fit the limits of course, but the arched neck and raised tail (that when it is not raised sweeps the ground) are authentic *cheval de Spanie*.

"He moves well," the blacksmith says with a smile. "All you have to do is *ride* him."

Nodding, I smile because George's history is quite clear to me now. It began in Spain when Hannibal imported Arabian stallions to improve the Celtic horse blood. With a little imagination, I can see Hannibal on George's busy back. He is the first Spanish horse born to be ridden seventeen hundred years later by the conquistadors in America. George, quite plainly, has the blood of El Morazillo (the horse that Cortez rode to his death and deification by the Indians) in his veins. He is the horse for which King Richard would have given his kingdom — and I have waited, perhaps, all of my life. "A good broke western horse," the blacksmith says.

And I say, as I have often said before, "*Tomorrow*, I'll ride him."